PETER HUTSON-JONES

Jacob's Dory

a novel

Enjoy my Book

www.peterhutsonjones.com

For Andrea, Freya and Cathy, with love.

Acknowledgements

Thanks, as ever, to the entire team at Electric Reads, particularly Sara, for the skill and sensitivity employed during edit.

Thanks also to the people who befriended me in the town of Mahone Bay, Nova Scotia. I was very fortunate to live in this wonderful corner of the world, albeit for too short a time.

And finally, to Skipper my wonderful Airedale terrier who would accompany me, whatever the weather as I walked along the Atlantic coastline in search of inspiration.

Sable Island 1869

1

Bow

JACOB MADDER CROUCHED BEHIND THE BROKEN, sun-bleached remains of a small wooden fishing boat protruding from the earth. This had been the late Archibald Tanner's working dory. Jacob's hiding place was on the very south-western tip of Sable Island; the landscape was wild, rugged, and seldom visited by the islanders. He hoped that his presence here would not be easily detected. He had arrived, out of breath from his hasty escape, just as the winter sun threw out its final, meagre shreds of warmth. The early evening chill had now started to attach itself to his young, vulnerable skin. The icy fingers of the brutal Atlantic wind had him firmly in their grip. He was woefully underdressed due to the speed of his departure, and he now longed for the warmth of his heavy overcoat, which hung redundantly on the wooden peg beside his front door.

The isolation had begun to gnaw at his very being. He stared blankly at the wooden bow that towered above him, following its rough outline, noting the torn, splintered edges, only apparent this close up. He recalled the only other time he had been this near to the wooden pillars. He had been much younger, perhaps six or seven years of age, when everything he did seemed fun. Now, ten years later, he wondered if he should have paid more attention to the stories recounted by the fishermen as they sat near the dock repairing their damaged nets. He felt ashamed that he knew so little of the fables of South Shore and her lost fishermen. This, however, paled in comparison to the shame he felt for what he had done earlier that afternoon.

Jacob had no idea who it was that had first noticed that the transom of a dory resembled a tombstone; perhaps it was the boat builders themselves as they pieced together the various wooden components – including the semi-circular stern section - that made up the finished craft. Nor did he know who it was that had decided to hammer parts of the broken boats into the unforgiving earth, along the precipitous headland of South Shore. Whoever it had been, these pillars, made from the broken boats, had become a fitting tribute to the island's lost mariners. Some of the oldest timbers were close to a hundred years old. It was safe, therefore, to assume that it must have been the earliest settlers on Sable who decreed this place appropriate for a memorial to those lost at sea. It was a place that wives and mothers could visit – a monument to the men and boys who did not come home, despite the fact that all islanders knew there were no actual bones lying under the rocky skin of South Shore. All were lost as part of the great ocean's regeneration. Flesh and skin removed by hungry sea life, and the bones left to be harvested by the bottom-dwelling inhabitants of the Atlantic.

The older islanders believed that placing the shattered boats directly into the ground so close to the shoreline somehow reconnected their unfortunate owners to Sable Island, post an oft-terrible demise. They had named this place "The Field of Souls", and the sound of air squeezing through the decaying timbers resembled, to young Jacob, the ghostly moans and groans of the dear departed.

As Jacob waited, his thoughts wandered to the last time he had actually seen Archibald Tanner. As is often the case in small communities, he had known the burly fisherman by sight; in fact, he knew the names of all the fishermen working on the island. It was literally a year to the day, on a typical October morning, when he had last spied Tanner, who, absorbed in his task of loading nets, traps, and baited long lines into his small dory, did not notice the fifteen-year-old boy watching his every move. Jacob, under strict instruction from his father, had been at the dock well before dawn, as the early morning mist covered the bay like a spider's web.

Jacob was a slight boy of fair complexion, with the most startling green eyes. Most people who met him made a point of saying how attractive he was. And yet, his wiry frame and youthful appearance was considered by the fishermen on Sable to be "unsuitable for fishing the unforgiving seas that surround the Maritimes". Jacob had a mop of blond hair that his father felt he wore too long –

but on account of his late wife's wishes, he had not insisted on his son wearing his hair short. Jacob's mother, herself a bird of a woman, had dressed her only son in clothes more suitable for a girl as he'd grown up. She had spent many hours combing her child's hair as if he was a doll, and in his formative years, when the family lived in Halifax, Jacob was often mistaken for a young girl. Nevertheless, he was well-liked by everyone who made his acquaintance. He had a most infectious personality and was instantly adored, especially amongst women.

Tom Madder – Jacob's father – was determined that his son would become a good fisherman and, hair apart, was very tough on the boy. He had, at great expense, taken delivery of a twenty-three foot long dory with full sail. Dories such as Tom Madder's were only recently being made, in Massachusetts, and there were only a few men in the province who could have afforded to have such a boat commissioned. The boat had only been in the water once, just after delivery, and as such needed only modest maintenance. However, Tom Madder instructed his son to walk the length of East Street to the main dock on a daily basis, whatever the weather, and clean the boat. It was his vain hope that a spark would be ignited within Jacob, who would grow to love the idea of fishing from such a fine boat. Unfortunately, the repetitive chore had only dampened any enthusiasm Jacob may have held for being out on the water.

The fishermen, who, with much hilarity, watched young Jacob tend to the big boat, held the thought that if he did in fact take to sea he would most likely be thrown overboard and drown. These men only whispered such thoughts out of earshot of Tom Madder – they knew that if any criticism was heard they would pay in one way or another. After a few short weeks of observing Jacob the fishermen had lost interest in his daily chores and had returned to their own hardworking ways.

Jacob silently observed the big fisherman push his fully-laden vessel out into the bay. A loon let out its mournful song as Tanner's oars dipped gracefully into the water. Tanner began to gently propel his boat towards what would be his last ever day of fishing. Jacob did not realise that his green eyes would be the last to see Archibald Tanner alive.

The bay was unusually still for October. With not a breath of wind fighting Tanner's passage, his dory slowly disappeared into the eerie mist. Jacob strained his eyes to see the pale blue dory fade from sight. The sea seemed to sway in a gentle hypnotic roll that made Jacob feel sleepy. Even the loon bobbing gracefully on the surface of the ocean seemed at ease, as it let out another melancholy cry.

It had been a busy morning, as was usual on fishing days, yet Tanner had managed to find a small window of time to pray. Not that he was the religious type – unlike some on Sable, who would not even move if the Lord seemed against it – but today was a day when he could use all the help he could get, and if God was listening then this was the time to let it be known.

Sable Island – being located just a few miles off the coast

of the Canadian Eastern seaboard – held limited guarantees when it came to prosperous fishing. A fisherman, no matter how skilled, would likely be greeted with danger as he navigated the treacherous waters that surrounded the island. To be an Atlantic fisherman was a precarious profession. Tanner, who had fished these waters since he was a boy, was not immune to these dangers; and he didn't know any schooner captain foolhardy enough to set sail in late October. The rich fishing off the Grand Banks had ended in September, and now the men would have to wait until the schooners set sail again in spring. They would have to be content with off-shore fishing using long line with baited hooks and the laying of lobster pots out of season, which was back-breaking work.

Fishing these waters had become much harder in recent years. The number of schooners heading for the rich grounds off of Newfoundland had reduced dramatically. In the last five years alone, the number of schooners, each with ten two-man dories on deck, had fallen from over forty-five to just eight. In simple terms, there were now more fishermen with their dories than places available on the great sailboats heading for the Grand Banks. If you were one of the unlucky fishermen not chosen to work on one of the eight, you had to either rely on inshore fishing year round or give up altogether and head for the towns and cities in search of alternative employment.

Fish stocks themselves had also started to disappear alarmingly. Joshua Mouton, the oldest fisherman on Sable, was always saying, in his deep, gravelly voice, "For some reasons never explained to me, the salt water around our country has become hostile to fish life. When I was a young man, the water in these parts was perfectly clear. Why, you could see the bottom even at twenty fathoms. Now my nets come up covered in shitty slime, how can fish exist in that?" the old salt would moan.

Jacob and his good friend Eli James, like all children on the island, were very frightened of Old Joshua; he reeked of fish oil and pine. He was missing all of his teeth and three fingers on his right hand – an old fishing injury. The wounds had healed, twisted in such a way that made the remaining digits terrifying to a child. Old Joshua would sit at the end of the dock in Freetown, crouched over his bait buckets, frightening the youngsters at every available opportunity. He considered this act part of his occupation and seemed to relish his employment.

Fishing in the Maritimes in the late 1800's was a delicate balance between profit and loss, and the results for individual Sable fisherman were too often debt and impoverishment. It was a tough existence, that only the very determined or the very lucky could endure. Many of the men of the province were the sons of individuals who had become fishermen by accident. The earth on the eastern mainland of Nova Scotia was generally so poor that agricultural-based professions were limited, but the earliest settlers had found the waters around the island a viable proposition; so rich with life that they were able to make a good living with only modest skill and effort.

Archibald Tanner had just completed the poorest fishing season he could ever remember and as a direct result was not only well behind with his rents, but had turned to more risky waters in a bid to make up the deficit. Laying traps out of season was not the answer, as even during high season from mid-April to July a fisherman would earn a paltry forty–five cents for a haul of one hundred lobsters. In October, sudden changes in wind or currents added to an already incredibly risky occupation.

Tanner asked himself, "Why has this life become so hard?" He was an honest man who lived with only good intentions. From the day that he had stepped onto the deck of the schooner "The Alice Dawn" alongside his father, he had had no choice in his profession. His father had fished all of his own life, "since birth", many would be heard to say. Tanner senior would tell his son, "Fishin' is in Tanner blood. Why, if they cut us, boy, we would bleed saltwater."

Archibald was now in the grip of a vocation that was not only on the verge of ruining him but the very cusp of killing him.

Not one man, woman, or child born in the Maritimes would have predicted that Archibald Tanner, who was after all a very experienced inshore boatman, would cast his lines just off Martin's Point, alone in his dory. Here he was though, fighting the rising swell with one grip whilst hauling lines with the other, his foot firmly wedged beneath the footboard.

"Where are you, fish?" Tanner cried above the sound of water hitting rock. "Damn you, I know you're down there. Jesus Christ, can you tell these fish to bite!?" He was now shouting at the top of his voice above the tempest that had suddenly hit Martin's Point. If anyone had been standing on the headland they would not have believed the weather could change so quickly, but this was the reality of island life.

Suddenly, his right hand, holding in place the baited long line, could feel the weight of fish. "Ha, that's it boys, grab a hold." The fish were directly below his boat, and he could sense exhilaration rising within his body. He knew he was too close to the rocks, yet his rising adrenalin made him ignore the danger; he would not abandon the line with its payload. The boat lurched violently, and Tanner nearly lost his balance; only his great skill, honed from years in a dory, allowed him to remain upright in such a fiercely bobbing boat. However, he needed both hands to steer the vessel away from disaster, yet couldn't let this catch go. It was too important, and he was too stubborn to let the silvery jewels attached to his line return to the dark water.

Tanner was now gripping the tiller so hard that any movement of the dory resonated through his tightening muscles. He was fighting a great beast, a dark demon; surely God would come to save him in his hour of need? A large swell hit his dory so hard that it turned the small boat round fully, sending it directly towards the rocks. He was just feet away from hitting the stone between land and sea head on. The bow of the boat cut a course so true that his only hope was to abandon both his line and the boat itself.

He looked at the dark, foaming water slapping wildly against the boat's transom, as he tried to plot his escape. Standing precariously upon the transom, he could make out yet more deadly forms just under the surface, as if the ocean was a boiling cauldron of chowder – rising and falling – reaching out to pull him under, to a watery end. The rocks glistened as a sliver of sunlight broke through the angry sky. Tanner felt as if a light had been shone directly at the spot that was to be his entry into the raging torrent. He braced himself, ready to dive in and make good his escape. But his hesitation meant that it was already too late.

A large cracking noise signalled that the boat had run aground. The bow, in one inglorious movement, broke away from the rest of the boat, to be thrown high into the salt-laden air. It landed some thirty feet above sea level, high on the rocky outcrop, where the smaller parts of the broken boat disappeared into the uneven surface of the cliff face. The bow itself was left lying, intact, upon the great mass of stone. Tanner was similarly thrown out, headfirst, over the boat's transom, landing firmly face down on top of a pointed rock. It pierced his head with such force that it protruded through the back of his skull. The jagged edge of the rock entered his head through his left eye socket, exiting through the wet hair just behind his right ear. Blood oozed into the sea, instantly lost, diluted as part of one great pool of liquid. His body was left lifelessly dancing with the will of the waves, like a puppet controlled by strings of seaweed and splintered wood.

So it came to pass that Archibald Tanner died that chilly October morning. The bow of his boat was hauled up the cliff by the islanders, to be placed alongside other memorials protruding out of the earth on the weather-ravaged strip of Sable Island. Now, one year later, as Jacob hid behind the dory, he ran his fingers along the crudely-etched name on the wood. "A Tanner – taken by the sea, October 26th, 1868." His index finger left the coarse indentations as he considered what fate waited for him following the day's events and if he would ever be remembered as he himself recalled Tanner the fisherman.

2

The Pain of Nancy Haas

IT MUST HAVE BEEN JUST AFTER six in the afternoon when for one brief moment, Nancy Haas felt normal, free to consider that she may be able to actually leave this place. Then the pain returned. She lay on her side with her eyes closed, trying with all the will she could muster to imagine the stars, bright in the Nova Scotia sky. She hoped this image would comfort her as she trembled with fear and pain. She wanted to transport her mind to another place, to find a box in a corner of a dream that she could hide in.

Her salty, soft skin, now fully exposed below the waist, was covered in small bumps where each tiny pore made her down-like hair stand up in an effort to preserve heat. A slight smell of ammonia flooded her nostrils, making her feel as if she would throw up at any moment. The skin around her thigh was irritated by the dampness caused by her unwitting urination.

"Mommy, please help me, please come," she cried aloud, keeping her eyes firmly closed. She felt that if she could not register her surroundings, see the wood pile in the corner, look at the rusting shovel hanging from an old nail on the wall behind the toilet, she would be safe.

"Don't look, don't look," she whispered, as tears streamed down her cheeks, before dropping gently into the dust and dirt that covered the floor. "What you can't see won't hurt you," she recalled. They were words her mother had once said.

Nancy knew the possibility existed he would return shortly. All of her being wanted to escape, to find a hiding place where he could not find her. He had tied her well with thick gauge fishing line, and any movement forced the line deeper into her delicate skin. Reddish marks had formed on her wrists and ankles. There was no escaping, no running away.

Her knees were bloodied and raw from where she had been dragged to the wooden outhouse. The path between the main house and this outside toilet storeroom was rough. Jagged stone and damaged roots were prevalent and had dug into her legs as he hauled her against her will to where she now lay, trussed up on the floor. She had noticed, as he dragged her, the small pond that ran adjacent to the path. Being late October, it was cold, the pond just frozen, and broken branches caught in the ice reached out of pond like the arms of drowning men trying to be saved, or perhaps trying to save her.

She was finding it increasingly hard to breathe. Her every breath came shallower than the last as she tried to swallow. She could taste the sea in a very unpleasant way. A light was fading in Nancy. Her chest was constricted as if in the grip of a great serpent, and she longed to rip it open, to once again take a drink of clean air. The object that he had stuffed into her throat completely obstructed her airway, and a faint gurgling sound replaced her normal respiration. A long thread irritated the back of her throat and as she struggled to inhale it became worse. She began to drift in and out of consciousness, the usual clarity of her thoughts obliterated by waves of agony. She was in a desperate situation and she knew it. Loud footsteps were approaching the outhouse, she knew he had returned to finish what he had started. A short moment's silence before the door flew open. Nancy closed her eyes as she realised the end of her life was near. Silently she prayed, hoping that she would be reunited with her mother. She was afraid no more.

Nancy had walked to the Madder home earlier that afternoon on the invitation of her good friend, Jacob. She had taken East Street, wearing her thick red shawl held together at the front by the pewter sand dollar broach her mother had given her. She never went anywhere without the broach; it was the last gift her mother had bestowed to her. She was generally in good spirits and excited that the school day had ended so early.

Nancy, who was a very bright girl, found some of the work set by the schoolteacher, Miss Roberts, too easy. The temporary post held by the elderly spinster had been temporary for the last ten years, and in all probability she would pass away before a permanent hiring could be made. A lack of students on the island ensured that a quick appointment was not on the horizon. Besides, the adults liked the old woman.

Miss Roberts, despite approaching her seventy-fifth year, had made a valiant attempt at providing a sound education to the island's children for years. Upon joining the modest seat of education, she had found that a lot of the children could not cope with even basic elementary studies. However, under the old-fashioned tutelage of Ida Roberts, they now left school able to read and write to an acceptable standard.

The large classroom – situated within Nancy's home, Dove House – catered to children of all ages. The class of 1869 had a total of nine students, six of whom were under ten and could barely read. Nancy, Jacob, and Eli James – the son of the lighthouse keeper – also attended. Miss Roberts found it a constant struggle to challenge the teenagers while keeping the attention of the infants. The younger students were a handful for the old teacher and were in need of constant supervision as they swarmed around the doddery educator.

Nancy was often entrusted to instigate projects for the two older boys, who both had a crush on the beautiful young girl. Having always loved reading, Nancy was considered by Miss Roberts to be the best candidate to tutor the boys in their final year of studies. Her favourite topics often related to faraway places; her thirst for knowledge on all matters geographical was unquenchable. Much to the two boys' annoyance, she would throw forth a barrage of questions on a daily basis.

"What is the most common crop exported from Mexico? What is the capital of France?" she would ask.

"Beans and Montreal," Eli would reply, knowing that his answers would send Nancy into a rage. He knew they were most probably wrong. Yet he did not know the correct ones.

"I give up on you two. You know nothing away from this island and are just plain stupid."

"Yeah, yeah all right," Jacob said, fully aware that Nancy would never give up on them, she liked them too much.

Today, Miss Roberts had been tired and feeling slightly under the weather. She had already escorted the younger children home to be under their mother's feet. The older three had fared for themselves and were now free to leave. Jacob had suggested that Nancy and Eli come to his house to try his father's latest home-brew. He knew his father would not miss one jug of the strong elixir, having made a substantial amount, and he was interested to see how the alcohol affected both Eli and Nancy.

"Are you coming, Nance?" asked Jacob, as both boys put on their coats.

"Yes, I will follow you two in a little while. I want to finish something. Is that alright?"

"We shall start drinking without you, then. Dad will be home around six so make sure you come before so you can have a drop, if there's any left!"

The two boys left together. It was just after one in the

afternoon.

Nancy sat back and found that she enjoyed the quietness of the house now that Miss Roberts and all the students had gone. In many ways, she had grown accustomed to the noise associated with study and prayer. She had grown up to the sound of hymns and laughter. Yet at this moment, she appreciated the calm. Besides, it gave her a little time to read, without interruption.

What Nancy really wanted was to finish reading Anna Maria Falconbridge's "Narrative Of Two Voyages", which Miss Roberts had kindly lent her. The book covered letters of Falconbridge's experiences travelling in West Africa from 1791 to 1793. The writer had sent the letters to a friend in England and a book of them had been published to great acclaim. Nancy felt that she was a most remarkable woman, to have carried on with her journey alone, especially since her husband had died under suspicious circumstances. Nancy had also never heard of Sierra Leone, let alone understood the slave trade, so found the book fascinating.

Being a relatively short book, Nancy had finished it well before four o'clock. She always felt a sense of sadness when she finished a book, as if she had lost a part of something she cared about.

With a huge sigh, she placed the book back onto Miss Roberts' desk and put on her red shawl, shutting the door behind her to head up East Street and towards Jacob's house.

3

Tom Madder's Outhouse

BY THREE O'CLOCK JACOB AND ELI had already finished two glasses of the hooch and were beginning to act stupidly when Nancy had arrived at the corner of Young and East Street. Her firm knock was greeted with a few giggles from inside the house.

"Shut up, Jacob," Eli whispered, "Let's scare her."

"What?"

"Be silent and wait until I have hidden upstairs."

"Huh?"

"You're such an idiot, Jacob Madder. You answer the door and tell Nancy that I went home, ok?"

Eli stumbled up the stairs, waiting in the small recess just outside of Jacob's bedroom. Though the light was poor, he had a clear view of downstairs.

"Hi Nance, come in." Jacob's face was flushed due to the alcohol.

"Where's Eli?"

"Oh, he had to go home early, something to do with helping his dad with the lighthouse, I think."

"Right, so what have you two been up to without me?"

Nancy knew Jacob was lying and she scanned the house beyond his shoulder, looking for signs of Eli.

She did not take off her red shawl, clinging to its comfort as she pushed past Jacob. She paused, smiling as she noticed how much taller than Jacob Madder she had become. They were the same age, yet Nancy – as girls often do – seemed so much older.

She knew Eli would be hiding somewhere in the house. It was a game they always played and was beginning to become tiresome. Eli was at least six inches taller than Nancy and about twice her bodyweight and as such she would hear him if he attempted to move. During their formative years, Eli was always the leader. His jet black hair was worn slicked back, highlighting a large forehead above steely eyes and angular cheekbones. He was self-assured, some thought cocky, and most of the older inhabitants on Sable did not like him. They thought him to be not only arrogant but also a mummy's boy, knowing how Mrs James constantly fussed both her husband and son in public.

Lisbeth James was a powerful woman. Attractive, in a manly way, with well-defined, muscular limbs, and a very pretty face sat atop a solid figure used to the rigours of hard work. She considered her profession to be pushing her weak husband forth and nurturing her son. It was commonly known – as most things are on a small island – that she ran the James household. Even though she was strict with regards to Eli's upbringing, she was ferociously protective of her young son. He could do no wrong, and when he did, she would excuse his behaviour and instead apportion the blame elsewhere.

"Nancy, you've got to try my dad's hooch." Jacob wore a stupid grin that Nancy found abhorrent. She was unused to thinking bad things about Jacob Madder but today she felt irritated by his infantile behaviour.

"I will not like it, you know that. I do not want to be in trouble with your father, Jacob, and I know you should think the same."

"Go on, Nancy, it's not half as bad as you think and it makes you happy." Jacob seemed excited and obviously wished he could share this new experience.

Nancy had always held a soft spot for Jacob, perhaps due in part to them both having lost their mothers at an early age. They would often just talk, about anything and everything. They usually felt comfortable in each other's company and were frequently seen together simply sitting on the main dock, deep in conversation. Nancy was always mature for her age and in the last few months her body had begun to catch up. She looked older than her years and as such had started to gain the attentions of several of the younger fishermen on the island.

Eli was slowly moving to the head of the stairs as he drained the cup of moonshine he had been holding in his right hand – his third cupful intensified the warm feeling in his throat.

"You may as well come down, Eli. I know you're there." Nancy didn't even glance up as she passed the stairwell and sat down in front of the fire. On the table was a large jug of Tom Madder's homebrew, stopper removed. It was already half-empty.

Jacob had never drunk before. This new intoxication fuelled his confidence and he sat, suddenly aware of Nancy's budding breasts. He longed to touch her. She had now taken off her shawl and placed it over the back of the chair next to hers. Nancy was wearing her old cream shirt, which was a little too tight. She had forgotten to change into the new one, which she had only just finished, and, noticing Jacob looking directly at the gaping buttons, she became a little self-aware and uncomfortable.

A strange tingle grew in Jacob's groin, and he liked it. He was sitting directly opposite the young girl and poured a large cup, which he pushed across the table. A small amount of the liquid spilled onto the table-top. Eli, who had now come downstairs, quickly reached over Nancy's shoulder, running his fingers through the wet trail then rubbing his teeth with his damp index finger, making a gentle squeaking noise. Nancy looked up at him, rolling her eyes in disdain.

"Go on Nance, have a swig."

"No, Jacob. I will only try it when I feel like it." Nancy was beginning to dislike Jacob's newfound confidence. His insistence was starting to become annoying.

"Nancy is scared, Jacob, she's such a girl," Eli said.

"Of course I'm a girl you dimwit, or perhaps you haven't noticed?" Nancy was beginning to feel that she should have stayed at home. Eli was annoying her with his usual arrogance and Jacob was just plain stupid due to the drink.

"Oh, I can see you're a girl, Nancy, and we sure have noticed your new additions," Eli said, licking his lips as he stared at her.

Reluctantly, she brought the cup to her lips, her nose scrunching up as the heady odour sprinted into her nasal cavity. As if about to taste something unpleasant, Nancy pinched just below the bridge of her nose as she drank.

"That's horrible, Jacob," she said, swallowing rapidly, the air laden with the smell of burning wood. Eli and Jacob started to laugh.

"Show her how it's done Jacob. You and me shall finish this jug."

Jacob stopped laughing; he suddenly started to feel strange. Without a word, he got up and headed towards the small kitchen. His mouth began to fill with a watery liquid and he needed to get outside, quickly. Grappling with the simple door-handle, he left the house and headed out into the small garden. The door bounced off the latch as it slammed shut.

"Where do you think you're going?" Eli shouted after him, "We should finish this together, or are you a girl too, Jacob Madder?"

Back inside the house, awkwardness grew. Nancy did not like being left alone with Eli.

"I need to pee," she stated, with uncharacteristic bluntness, as she too headed for the back door. Nancy paused to unhook the small lantern that hung on the wall beside the door. Striking one of the matches gathered in a pile on a shelf, she lit the light with a single strike and went outside.

"No problem, you two lightweights. Can you hear me? I am going home, this is no fun anymore. Goodbye to the two of you!" Eli shouted at the top of his voice as he got up. He really didn't appreciate being left alone and decided it was time to seek out another game to play.

The outside toilet of the Madder house was cold and dark. Nancy placed the lantern on the floor by her feet. She quickly removed her under-garments and sat down on the uncomfortable wooden seat. In her haste, she had forgotten to close the door properly.

A man stood there, in the doorway, a terrifying dark vision. He was breathing hard, staring at Nancy as she sat frozen with fear. She was unable to make out the features of his face due to a lack of good light. Slowly, he moved towards her, kicking over the lantern, then in one movement lifting her up. She could smell a familiar mustiness on his coat as he lowered her to the floor. This shadow man mesmerised and terrified her. As if paralysed, she seemed incapable of fighting back.

He began to fumble with her shawl, pulling at it in a frenzied attempt to reach her bare skin. As he tore at the shawl, her pewter broach sprung open and rolled into the darkness of the outhouse. She let out a cry, her first sound since he had arrived. She wanted to fight now, as if the potential loss of her mother's gift galvanised her will.

Moving with greater urgency, he straddled her slender body, freeing his hands to claw at her remaining clothes. As her blouse fell open she could hear him let out a gentle moan. He reached her bare bosom. Fumbling at her nipples with his fingers, he rubbed across her areola with his thumb.

Nancy found an inner strength as he ran his hand between her legs. She brought her knees up and started kicking violently. He slapped her hard and she screamed, and then screamed again. Panicking, he thrust his other hand into his coat pocket, retrieving a ball of old fishing line.

"Shut up, just be quiet," he cursed. Nancy knew the voice immediately. "Why?" she hissed, and she began to scream as loud as she could.

"You can't, they will hear. Stop it now." He was starting to lose control. It wasn't meant to be like this. This was not how he had pictured it.

He stuffed the ball of line into her mouth, forcing it deep into her larynx. Beginning to cough, she tried to spit out the alien mass. Covering her mouth with the ripped blouse, he attempted to quell the guttural sound.

"Shush now, sweet girl. It will be all right, just be quiet. Please be quiet." He began stroking the side of her head, much like a mother would to settle a child.

Nancy went quiet; she had given up the struggle. Her body was limp, her face contorted. The fight had ended; a light had been snuffed out. Before he left to check if anyone in the house had been disturbed, he bound her hands with fishing line and then ripped some material from her blouse. He secured this, tying it in a bow behind her head, covering her mouth.

He hesitated, feeling confused. Perhaps he should take her back into the house, to bed. Say she was ill. It was not his fault. In his eyes, it was always somebody else's fault.

He started to drag Nancy along the stone path, then, half-way down, stopped. Looking up at the dark sky he let go of her and raised his hands to his head, starting to tap his temple on both sides.

"No, no this is not good, take her back to the outhouse," he muttered to himself, struggling to formulate a plan.

He turned back in the direction of the outhouse, reached down to grab Nancy, and proceeded to drag her back along the uneven path.

Shutting the door, he headed out again, this time, alone.

The door back into the main house was ajar, projecting a shard of light that pierced the gloom. As if he knew this route perfectly, he rapidly advanced through the kitchen and headed upstairs to the rear bedroom. He barely noticed the figure of a boy curled up like a large cat at the foot of the stairs. He needed to check if the rooms upstairs were empty. Once he had checked all the rooms he returned to the front bedroom and sat down on the edge of the small bed. Both of his legs involuntarily moved up and down causing a military type tapping on the wooden floor as he considered his options. Sweat had formed a glassy layer on his brow that he slowly wiped away with the palms of his hands. It was now six fifteen and he knew time was already against him.

His plan was simple; he just needed to steady his nerves. He must return to the outhouse and kill her. Surely, no-one would believe that it was he who had killed Nancy. That wouldn't happen, would it?

She didn't cry out as he moved through the house a second time, this time with Nancy in tow. The air in the house had changed; it had a different density than before and was now heavy and oppressive. He placed her carefully on the floor, rigid and cold. The shadow slowly removed his coat in front of her, carefully folding it up and then putting it over his arm. He paused for a brief moment to look down on Nancy, then left the room.

4

A Father's Promise

FEAR AND PANIC ARE TERRIBLE BEDFELLOWS, and the shame was almost too much for Jacob to bear. How could he have committed such a callous act? He had loved Nancy after all. He had already considered leaping from the bluff into the icy waters below, where, within minutes, he would be unconscious and the ramifications of his actions would be gone. He vomited. The salty product of his gentle sobbing soon replaced the acrid sour taste in his throat as tears reached the corners of his mouth. This gentle weeping gave way to great, heaving moans that made it hard for him to breathe. He wanted to sleep but found it impossible as his mind became overcrowded with all the events of earlier in the day. He could not make sense of the jumbled images flashing before him. His father's voice resonated in his head over and over, as if he had returned to that horrible place. "What have you done, Jacob, what have you done?"

Jacob held his eyes shut for just a few moments, but this only brought to mind the startling image of Nancy lying unnaturally on the wooden floor of his bedroom, her eyes still open, lifeless and glassy, her mouth contorted, filled with balled-up fishing line. A single streak of her youthful blood had trickled from her nose and dried on her skin like blistered paint on an old boat. He wailed at the thought of poor Nancy's last vision in life – was it Jacob, her friend, who she trusted, forcing himself on her?

Re-opening his eyes to escape the memories of the bruises and cuts on her upper thighs, Jacob slowly and painfully stood up, trying to clear his head and gain a better view of his surroundings. His hair was dirty and damp, sticky with Nancy's blood. Jacob looked at the palms of his small hands, which seemed to him like somebody else's. As he wiped the tears from his face using the collar of his shirt, the roughness of the dirty material chafed his already wind-burnt cheeks.

Fully standing, Jacob could only just make out the shadowy outline of the lighthouse in the distance. The failing light and seemingly horizontal precipitation made it feel to Jacob like he was trying to focus on an image by looking through sackcloth. Only the lighthouse's bright lantern was clearly visible, as though detached from the stone and mortar that held it in place. Imposing and solid, Sable End Lighthouse had stood on the south-western tip for more than a century, a permanent saviour for passing mariners. The island, though, was known as the graveyard of the Atlantic, due to the ever-present risk of the rocks that surrounded the main landmass.

The lighthouse stood at forty feet, having recently been rebuilt due to erosion of the bluff. The fixed white light was, since the reconstruction, fuelled by lard, having previously been kept alight using seal oil. Jacob knew that a select group – including his father – would be huddled inside, fully aware of what had happened to Nancy Haas. What he could not have known was that his father was in the process of outlining a promise to find his son and transport him to Lunenburg himself.

"All of you know me and that I be true to my word. Just give me this night and I will find the boy and take him to the mainland. My promise is that, and all I ask in return is that I do this alone as is my duty," said Thomas Madder, with such authority that it was unlikely anyone would question him. Following a long pause for consideration, the three other men present agreed.

Thomas Samuel Madder, or plain Tom Madder to everyone on Sable, was regarded as "The King of the Fishermen", although this was not because Tom fished. Indeed, he was not skilled at all on the water. The name had stuck after he arrived on the island ten years ago with wealth enough to ensure he was able to take advantage of the misfortune of others. During the great storms of '62, he profited as the hauls of all of Sable's fleet failed. The fishermen would have surely starved if not for the dubious financial assistance handed out by Madder. He traded cash for stakes in the boats and provided the loans used for renting equipment. The poor fishermen failed to meet unrealistic deadlines for repayments of said loans, with the net result being that Madder now owned a part of all fishing operations on the island. Madder was a large man, his frame inherited from his father. He wore his thick black hair in a unique style, swept dramatically across his forehead, covering his large ears in one bulbous clump.

According to the 1861 five island censuses, there were eighty-nine inhabitants of Sable Island, of who forty-two were hardy Acadian fishermen. Other islanders were employed to serve the three lighthouses as keepers or lifesavers. Tom Madder was either loathed or despised by them all. Even the sudden demise of his put-upon wife, Laura, during her second winter living on Sable didn't thaw any feelings towards Tom Madder. Most, though, felt sorry for his son – little Jacob.

Laura Settle had married beneath her family's expectations when she fell for Thomas Madder, the son of a dubious Halifax merchant. Her father, James, who had made his money from opportunities that arose during the early settlement of Nova Scotia had disowned her over her imminent marriage to Madder. Her mother, however, survived the powerful James Settle and when she in turn passed away, the family fortune was shared equally between Laura and her two brothers. Tom – who was well known for his frittering away of monies – set about re-appropriating her portion of the inheritance and had, within a very short time, gambled away almost half of it. They had set up home in the wealthy Boxborough district of the city and as there were, in that area, those determined to reduce the remaining funds, Madder decided to leave. In a moment of sheer impulsiveness, the Madders uprooted and left Halifax in a whirl. Furthermore, Thomas decided that the small island four miles off the coast of Lunenburg would be the ideal place to set up home, against Laura's wishes.

The wind continued to howl as it always did on the exposed headland, the remains of Tanner's boat providing Jacob only modest shelter from the elements. He needed time to understand what was happening to him, to process the awful truth. Unfortunately, time was against the boy as he waited. The heavy sky was beginning to release the first wet snow of the year; Jacob drew his arms tight around his chest whilst trying to see any movement emanating from the direction of the lighthouse.

Tom Madder left the lighthouse, pausing as he closed the door to tighten the belt holding his thick jacket closer to his large frame. The freezing air flooded his throat like drinking ice-cold water drawn straight from the well. Those left inside peered through the small window beside the door; this minor opening shed small amounts of natural light into the otherwise darkened lower floor of the lighthouse. Not a word was uttered as they tried to see Tom set about his task. The flickering candlelight deepened the shadows of the solemn faces pressed against the mottled glass, giving them a haunted appearance beyond their years.

The lighthouse's main beacon illuminated Madder as he drove on against the strong wind. His burly figure disappeared into the darkness as the big man left the elevated plateau that the lighthouse and keeper's residence were built on. There were seven large stone steps leading down onto the open ground between the buildings and South Shore, and only when he strode further away did his image reappear to those inside.

Eli James sat quietly against the outer wall of the stairwell that led up to the great beacon, observing the men with curiosity. They were still huddled around the window, straining to see Tom Madder. Eli was trying to remain as still as possible to avoid alerting anyone to his presence. His father, Robert – the lighthouse keeper – would have surely sent the boy across the courtyard to home and his mother. The men had actually forgotten that Eli was present and, much like a younger child, he was compelled not to move or speak to avoid warranting any attention. The conversation was about to hold some interest to Eli.

Realising that they could no longer follow Madder's pursuit, the three men left the window, each taking a place on mismatched chairs around the oak table directly in front of the fire. Franck Beck was the first to speak.

"This is a bad affair, gentlemen. That poor girl. How could this have happened on our island?" he said as he nervously tugged at a loose thread on the sleeve of his jumper.

Garrett Folcher always considered his words wisely; he was well known for the economy of his conversation, so much so that all listened to his minimal outpourings with greater interest. He took in a long, deep breath as he used the embers of the fire to re-light his old pipe. The others watched, spellbound, as he inhaled then exhaled a plume of grey smoke.

"Can we say that we trust Thomas Madder?" said Garrett. All the men present lurched forward in anticipation of him continuing, but Folcher sat back in his chair, returning his full concentration to the pipe.

Eli's father, Robert, had been keeping one eye on the proficiency of the lighthouse. With the athletic step of a much younger man, he skipped quickly up the narrow stairs, passing his son with ease. As an experienced lighthouse keeper, he was able to gauge the level of fuel left in the vessel below the light. Confident that his light would not be going out anytime soon, he was able to return to the lower floor. "So, what have we decided upon? What is the outcome of your machinations?" he said, giving off whiffs of irritation as strong as the smell of bad fish. Eli could tell that his father was agitated. He had seen this look on his father's face before and felt that perhaps the group should have waited before allowing Tom Madder to leave.

Seymour Johnson – an altogether nervous individual – said in his high-pitched voice, "I know it seems wrong to let a father help his son under such circumstances-"

"Catch his son," Robert James corrected, as a teacher would correct a pupil.

"Sorry, catch his son" said Johnson, slightly embarrassed, "but there has been too much sadness this day and I am sure Tom will deliver his son as was his promise. We have to trust him."

"Trust Thomas Madder? Good Lord, Seymour," said James, not hiding his disbelief at the assertion. "You ask any fisherman on Sable, no, ask any man in the Maritimes, if it is safe to trust Tom Madder!"

"I hope your faith is in the right place, Seymour," said Folcher, looking up from his pipe. "We all stand to be counted if it goes wrong."

"Someone has got to go to Dove House and let the reverend know. That is surely the thing we need to do. I would hate it if he heard from someone else," said Franck Beck. "I would go of course but you know my leg is sore and the journey would be…somewhat taxing," he continued.

Robert James rolled his eyes; it was well-known that Beck always used his ailments in a convenient manner. "I'll go," he said. "Seymour, can you keep an eye on the light? It should be fine for some hours as there is plenty of lard left ready to burn, but you never know. Oh, and Eli, be off to your mother," he added as he grabbed his coat, not casting one look at his son as he left. In truth, he wanted to leave; he did not care for the company sat around the table in his lighthouse. The prospect of telling Reverend Haas that his young daughter lay dead on the floor of Jacob Madder's bedroom was not something that he relished, but it had to be done and perhaps should have been done earlier.

Robert James left for Dove House. The modest building not only acted as the island's schoolhouse and communal place of worship, but was also the building called home by

Cole and Nancy, his only daughter.

As night fell on South Shore, the lighthouse cast its illumination so that Jacob only occasionally had a good view of the half-mile that lay between his hiding place and the foot of the great beacon. The light cast elongated shadows that exaggerated the gullies and rises of the space beyond.

With the light aiding his view, Jacob could make out a tall figure heading directly towards him. As quickly as he saw it, the figure disappeared, as it descended into a chasm. Jacob opened his eyes as wide as he could to try and penetrate the gloom, but to no avail. He could not as yet estimate the distance between him and the lone figure, but assumed it would not be long before he was discovered.

Jacob considered running to find another hiding place closer to the rocks, where, if necessary, he could climb down and remain out of sight. It would be dangerous, as at full tide all of the rocks would be covered with a slippery glaze. Maybe his pursuer would consider the search futile and give up? Somewhere deep within his heart he wanted to be found, for this anguish of being so alone in such an unforgiving place to be over.

He reached up to cup his ears, hoping to give himself some respite from the boom of the sea below, and was instantly aware that the whole of his head was numb. He could not feel anything, and his touch alerted him to the probability that he was in danger of freezing to death. He shook his head vigorously and looked out again in search of the figure heading towards him.

"Who are you?" he said aloud, his voice breaking into a staccato tone.

All sorts of possibilities clamoured for attention in Jacob's brain. Sharp pains began to rise within his pounding chest as he contemplated what was about to happen to him. The young boy was shaking so much that he was convinced his now uncontrollable state would give him away. He crouched down into a ball, somewhat resembling a large buoy, in the hope that the approaching figure would miss him altogether, would fail to spot him hiding behind Tanner's tombstone. He dared not move as the pursuer arrived and weaved in and out of the various broken boats.

Time seemed to stop altogether; only the hiss of large waves hitting the shore below defied the stillness in Jacob's mind. Holding his breath, Jacob braced himself for capture, tensing each of his young muscles and digging his fingernails into his soft palms. Minutes passed, and the thought occurred to him that he might actually evade the stranger. He slowly began to relax, raising his head to see if his pursuer had moved beyond the headland. As he looked out he became aware that he could see the sinister figure on the sand. It ghosted forward and stood directly before him. He was trapped, Tanner's bow behind and the man in front. He was unable to make out any of the features on the man's face, as it was now completely dark. In an instant, a large, gloved hand gained a firm grip on Jacob's collar, lifting the young boy clean off his feet. Jacob let out a strangled scream whilst flailing his limbs in a furious attempt to break free.

"Steady, boy," said Tom. Jacob was now in such a frenzied state that he did not pay heed to a voice he should have known. Even though Tom's grip was firm it was becoming increasingly difficult to maintain control of the situation. Jacob was kicking and screaming furiously, so much so that he might injure both of them.

Tom had to gain control by whatever means he could. Jacob must be calmed.

Whilst gripping the boy with one hand, the stranger brought his other gloved hand round in an arc, striking Jacob firmly across his temple. The force of the blow was so great that Jacob instantly passed out.

5

A Less Than Perfect Departure

AFTER A SHORT TIME, JACOB CAME round. Bewildered, he found himself sat up against the very same bow that he had been hiding behind. In front of him was his father, who, having lit a small travelling candle, was looking at his son sternly. Tom Madder spoke not a word as he reached down to lift his son onto his broad shoulders and headed purposefully in the direction of Freetown.

Being so late, it was dark enough that only those with intimate knowledge of the narrow paths that ran along the cliff's edge would be able to navigate a true route back to town. Even a tentative misstep would most certainly lead to disaster. Tom Madder strode on, sure of foot, only stopping briefly at regular intervals to catch his breath. Jacob, who was frightened beyond belief and wanted to walk rather than be carried as if he were a sack of potatoes, tried to speak.

"Father, please let me walk," Jacob said, his voice reverberating with nervous energy. "Put me down. I can walk!" he was shouting now. Tom Madder stopped. Perhaps concerned that Jacob would make a run for it, he reluctantly let his son slide, unceremoniously, to the ground.

"Stay close, Jacob. I warn you I will not let you be off."

During the final leg of their journey home, Jacob was desperate to ask his father what was to happen to him. He also wanted to know if his father was certain Nancy was dead. Having finally gained enough courage, he was able to spout forth a barrage of questions. Tom ignored these protestations and, upon each question, actually increased the pace, so much so that young Jacob, whilst trying to keep up, struggled to speak at all.

The house where Tom and Jacob Madder lived was on the corner of Young and East Street, Freetown, just a stone's throw from the main harbour. Given Madder's wealth it was a surprisingly modest abode, distinctly lacking in charm. Its position, however, gave Tom Madder a perfect view of the whole bay. From here he was able to keep check on the men who fished the waters using his equipment. During the season the fishermen would always look up East Street to ascertain if Madder was keeping watch, sat atop the widow's walk that had been constructed on the roof of the house. In truth, he rarely stood on the rook, but the thought that he could be there ensured the fishermen never lied to him about their hauls.

The shingles that covered the walls of the house had never been painted and were the familiar grey colour common on the island. Some were missing altogether, revealing the exposed, lighter wood beneath. The house was in total darkness as Tom turned the key in the solid door and pushed his way in. Jacob, like an obedient dog, followed at his father's heel.

The small garden to the front of the property was overgrown and untidy. For a short time when they had first moved in, Laura Madder had lovingly tended the plot. Neglect had arrived upon her demise and neither Tom nor Jacob was inclined to carry out any horticultural activities. The small picket fence that enclosed the property was similarly neglected; broken pieces of wood lay all around as if some passer-by had thrown driftwood collected on Freetown beach onto the plot.

Inside, the house felt cold and damp, matching Jacob's current mood. His father insisted that he sit and wait at the small table they ate from. Jacob's chin trembled and he wanted to cry, even though he knew this would further upset his father. Tom Madder was in the process of starting a fire in the open hearth as, without looking at his son, he spoke in hushed tones.

"I've got no choice, Jacob, what you've done cannot be undone, cannot be changed," his father began. His face looked grave as he continued. "We shall leave before dawn and head for Lunenburg - no, we shall head up the coast for Halifax. I shall deliver you to the Magistrate myself and we can tell him that you lost your mind – yes, that's what we will say." Tom Madder seemed indecisive as he delivered his words, as if he himself was a young boy formulating some excuse for a silly prank.

"You must get out of your wet clothes and I'll ready

everything we shall need for the sail," he said, with returning authority.

Without a word, Jacob undressed and headed for the stairs and his own room.

"Wait!" yelled his father, "You must not go up there! Stay here in front of the fire and I will fetch you some dry clothes."

Tom Madder often raised his voice to his young son, particularly in the years since Jacob's mother had passed away. Jacob froze at his father's command, his eyes firmly fixed to see if his father had removed his thick leather belt. He slowly retreated behind one of the wooden chairs, welcoming the space created between the two of them.

How could Jacob have forgotten what lay on the floor of his bedroom?

"Father, I'm so frightened," he said, as tears erupted, blown out in a great storm. He yearned for his dead mother. He wanted to be held, just a little warmth and contact from a loved one who would whisper to him that everything was going to be all right. In his heart, he knew that it would never be all right, life would never be the same. He was openly sobbing now, for Nancy, for his mother, and for himself. Tom wanted to hold his distraught son – but that would be weak. It was not a man's place to comfort the boy. Instead, he busied himself, first grabbing an assortment of Jacob's clothes then starting to prepare for the momentous day that lay ahead.

Once dressed, Jacob sat motionless, staring into the

embers of the fire. He was tired; his eyes, reddened and glassy, seemed transfixed by the dance of the flames. Jacob wore the complexion of a ghost.

The fire radiated a good deal of heat, allowing warmth to return slowly to his chilled body, his cheeks reclaiming their usual healthy, ruddy appearance. He once again looked normal. Only his eyes betrayed this illusion, looking forlorn and full of sorrow. He hadn't realized that he had put his sweater on back to front; these minor things held little importance on a day such as today. Nothing mattered anymore.

"We must sleep," his father said. "It will be a tough day tomorrow and we need our wits about us. The weather is set fair but could change, so I need you to lie down on my bed and get some rest, We have hard work before us." He knew full well that Jacob would not sleep for one moment tonight. He also knew that in order to navigate the full day's sail up the coast he would need his son to not be a liability aboard the dory.

Dutifully, Jacob silently headed for his father's bed. His weary limbs were painful and it took some effort to climb the stairs. The cold had penetrated his bones and now the chill of the upper floor meant it would be some time before he felt physically comfortable. Even the bed sheets were stone-cold as he slipped into the large bed, shivering. He wished that he could have stayed near the fire downstairs. The fire grate in the bedroom lay empty and unattended. He was too exhausted to build a fire himself, and now lay staring at the ceiling, waiting for sleep. Waiting, perhaps, for a nightmare.

It was half past four in the morning and Jacob was exhausted as he finally decided it was useless to even attempt sleep. He got out of his father's bed and, wrapped tightly in a fleece, stood at the window looking out at the stillness of the street. A little tabby cat was picking at a small pile of rubbish just outside the tatty front door of Joshua Mouton's cottage. The cat was a frequent visitor to East Street, where there was an abundance of treats to delve into and the odd rodent to chase. Jacob remained transfixed at the window for a further hour. It would not be long now before his father told him it was time to leave the island.

Meanwhile, Tom's preparations for the morning's sail were well under way. He had already packed salt pork, oat biscuits, and a cask of poteen into a large leather bag. Sealskin jackets lay atop coils of rope. There was also a large wooden trunk that contained additional clothing and other supplies. He planned to sail with speed for Halifax and time would not allow them to stop in Lunenburg or St Margaret's Bay. Tomorrow was Wednesday and he planned to sit in front of the constable on Thursday afternoon.

First light woke Tom Madder, who, having spent a restless night slumped in his mother's rocking chair, tried to stretch his aching shoulders into life. He rotated his neck and winced at the various cracking sounds emanating from his joints. He looked old this morning, as if he had aged ten years in one night. Peering from the large window that overlooked the bay, he could see that Freetown was still. Thankfully, the town remained asleep. He was pleased to note that the sky was pale blue, with only a touch of magenta welcoming dawn.

Bending down to pick up Jacob's clothes, still damp from the day before, a metallic thud diverted his attention. He balled the garments up, placing them untidily on one of the wooden chairs as he searched for the source of the noise. He could see a shiny broach against the dark floor. The unmistakable sand dollar shape, made from pewter. He picked it up to examine it. The broach was familiar; he just could not place when and where he had seen it. Tom couldn't recall ever seeing his wife wear such a broach and these days there were few female visitors to the house. With a sick feeling it dawned on him that it must belong to Nancy. It surely would be best to take it from the house and just get rid of it. The question of whether it had been in Jacob's clothes or if it had always been on the floor and had somehow got tangled within the garments would have to wait. Stuffing it into his deep pockets, he continued to get ready for the journey.

Within twenty minutes, the two of them were hauling the pile of provisions to be loaded onto Jacob's dory.

They were sailing away from Sable within the hour.

Three miles east of Sable, out at sea, a huge swell had started. The waves, now surging over twenty feet high, were being driven by a hurricane. The hurricane had been predicted in a letter sent to the editor of the London

Standard by Lieutenant Stephen Saxby, a Royal Navy astronomer, in November 1868, nearly twelve months earlier. The warning was ignored, the author considered a crackpot. The cyclone, however, was later named the Saxby Gale in homage to Lt. Saxby.

The storm would hit the coastline late the next day, on Wednesday afternoon, and high winds would batter the Eastern Seaboard of Nova Scotia for twenty-four hours. A transatlantic steamer had already felt the full force of the weather front and had sunk without being able to make any distress calls. Thirty-three people, crew and passengers, had entered the water and within two hours all were dead. In total, a further one hundred fatalities occurred in the Maritimes; winds reached one hundred and five miles per hour and tidal surges were in excess of fifty feet.

Unaware as Jacob and Tom were of the storm heading directly across the route the older man had set, they sailed on.

Jacob was distracted by the fate that awaited him. He expected little sympathy from the constable, who would surely put him in irons no matter what the circumstances. Unable to form his own memory of the events how could he then expect any stranger to question his guilt. He sat, stony-faced, looking towards the rear of the dory. He observed his father, who was occupied with maintaining a sound pace along the coastline.

Jacob was trying to piece together the events of the previous day. He just couldn't remember. He bemoaned drinking so much and knew that his own weakness had led him to this place. Eli had always been the stronger one, the one who made the decisions. Jacob now wished he had stood up to his friend. Perhaps Eli knew exactly what had happened? Jacob needed to talk to his friend as soon as he could. He vowed to get a message to Eli, even if he was to be incarcerated when they arrived on the mainland.

6

Jacob's Suspicions Begin to Mount

AS A BOY, JACOB HAD FEARED that he was a constant disappointment to his father. On the other hand, his mother had religiously encouraged him to be more confident, implying perhaps that he should ignore his father's continual badgering and concentrate on creating his own, unique course. To a young boy that was all well and good, yet he seemed unable to tune out his father's opinions. From an early age, he was destined to follow rather than lead.

On one frightful occasion when he was much younger, he had laid out a plan to impress his father. It was a simple plan that involved polishing the gold pocket watch that had been handed down to his father across three previous generations. The watch was a treasured possession and as such was kept in a mahogany cabinet next to Jacob's father's writing desk. It was seldom used, as his father – since living in a fishing community – rarely wore a suitable waistcoat to attach the timepiece to. And yet several times each year, Tom Madder would carefully unwrap the cotton cloth that surrounded the watch and spend a full Sunday afternoon judiciously polishing the shiny outer case.

The summer of 1860 had been full of turmoil for Jacob's father, who had to spend several stressful weeks traveling between Halifax and Sable Island to conclude a business deal that was essential to maintaining the prosperity of the Madder business. He was likely trying to limit further losses to his wife's estate. Such was the extent of his time away that he had neglected to tend to his beloved watch at all.

On one long, particularly tedious Sunday afternoon, Jacob found himself standing on his tiptoes, looking at the bundle containing the family heirloom. He decided that there was no better way to impress his father than to take over the responsibility of cleaning the watch. He knew little of the mechanics of a pocket watch and how delicate they were. His little hands applied pressure on the case. It flipped out of his hands like a bar of soap, landing squarely on the stone floor. He quickly reached down to pick it up, and recoiled in horror as both the glass face and the gold back of the watch fell apart. Placing the three parts back into the cotton cloth, he returned it to the cabinet and fled from the house.

His father returned home two days later, but it wasn't for another two weeks that he found the time to clean the treasured watch.

"Jacob," his voice boomed through the house. "Get here this instant."

Tom Madder tore into his son as violently as if he had

found one of his employed fishermen stealing from his back pocket. The boy openly sobbed as he stood terrified and unsure of what to say or do. His father told him he was a disgrace and not fit to be a Madder. He then made his only son stand in the corner of the kitchen for several hours. Jacob's mother was angry with her husband and didn't agree with what she considered a complete overreaction – Jacob was only eight, after all.

"The boy has to be shown discipline." Tom would say.

As a caring mother, Laura's heart broke at the thought of her little Jacob being tormented by a bully of a father.

Humiliation complete, Jacob vowed never to help his father again, and the relationship continued to be fraught with tension for the rest of Jacob's childhood. It was not helped by Tom Madder occasionally turning to his belt to admonish his son.

Now, on the night of Nancy's murder, Jacob's dory cut a steady path through the waves. Fortunately for Tom Madder, the storm heading towards them was still some way off. The slick lines of the beautifully-engineered boat ensured that, in spite of being still further out from the coastline than he would have liked, Tom was able to manoeuvre the dory easily.

At the far end, towards the bow, Jacob sat deep in thought. He was not looking at all well, which was to be expected under the circumstances. He vowed never to drink again. He was racking his brains to think, to remember one fragment of his lost memory. He wondered how on earth so many of the fishermen on Sable could spend hours drinking so much yet still be seen pulling away at dawn for a day spent far out to sea. He also pondered; could you really do something you were completely unaware of? That thought terrified him.

"Why did you drink so much of my grog, Jacob? What were you thinking about?"

Jacob didn't so much as look at his father, who, wanting to talk, moved to the seat alongside his son. The dory gently rocked as Tom adjusted his weight to balance the boat. Tethering the tiller so that he could maintain the right bearing, he looked straight ahead as he continued.

"Did you talk Nancy into something she didn't want to do? Or was it that you were a bit curious about the differences between – you know what I mean. She was always a pretty one, Nancy." He was trying to be careful with his choice of words but whatever he said seemed to come out wrong. "I had to move her, you know. She was in a terrible state when I got home and you were in such a mess, and naked."

As any adolescent would be when talking about such matters with a parent, Jacob was totally embarrassed. Yes, he did think Nancy was beautiful, and she made him feel a certain way. But the thought that his own father thought she was pretty was disgusting. He just couldn't remember anything after passing out.

"I mean, she was lovely, was Nancy, well-developed for her age, why wouldn't you start to think of her as a woman? Listen, Jacob, I know that you consider yourself grown up, but you have so much to learn. Women can be so complicated and this is such a mess. I never talked to you about these things. I do understand how desire can make you feel...frustrated."

This was becoming excruciating for Jacob to hear and he started to think perhaps his father knew more about what had happened to Nancy than he was letting on.

"Can we just leave it till we get to the mainland? I don't want to talk about it anymore."

"Okay, son. I just want to help, that's all. You know, get our story straight before we come before the constable." Tom returned to the back of the boat, pausing as he adjusted the lines attached to the tiller, to look up at a menacing sky that all of a sudden seemed too close and a little threatening.

7

The Grief of Cole Haas

ROBERT JAMES HESITATED AS HE APPROACHED the front door to the Haas residence. The vibrant colour of the painted wood was at odds with the sober hues on the doors of the other houses flanking East Street. Robert had rehearsed his lines out loud for the whole duration of his grim walk from the lighthouse. Yet no amount of rehearsing would help, and as he stood on the stone threshold, the words he needed to say seemed jammed in his throat. Robert James knew full well that periods of mourning were frequent on Sable. Islanders, however, were not familiar with grieving for someone taken by something other than the hands of the sea. He dreaded what he knew would happen, the outpouring of grief, the pure grief of Cole Haas. He knocked, gently at first, on the large wooden door and waited.

Inside, Cole Haas was trying to write an appropriate sermon for this Sunday's service. He had been engrossed in this and other administrative tasks for hours. Time had simply slipped away, and he suddenly realised that outside, the light had gone and night had arrived.

These were tough times and with winter fast approaching, he needed to capture the words that could inspire a congregation made up almost entirely of fishermen. He looked down at the many pieces of scrunched-up paper balls lying about his feet. He then brought his gaze to the paper on top of his desk, with his latest words, scrawled by his own hand, upon it. Deciding to read them out loud to see if they struck a chord, he cleared his throat and began.

"Our great Maker intended the work to be hard; the tests we have to bear are extreme. I know the road we now travel upon will be rocky, yet the Lord shall reward us, those who truly believe." He hated it. It was condescending; who was he to preach in such a manner? Screwing it up, he tossed it away, to join the pile on the floor.

"Cole? Cole Haas, are you inside?" Robert shouted from beyond the front door, knocking louder this time. Cole was finally put out of his misery, his writing abandoned for the evening.

Carefully returning his pen to the well-worn groove next to a blackened, almost burnt-looking inkwell, he pushed his chair back and made for the door. As the tempo of the knocking increased, he hurried along, eager to answer his impatient caller.

"Yes, yes I can hear you Robert," he said as he opened the door.

"Good evening Cole, may I come in?"

Cole noticed that Robert did not look him in the eye as he spoke. He also noted that his visitor, normally a confident fellow, seemed shy, perhaps hesitant.

"Of course, Robert, please come in. Can I get you something hot to drink? You look cold."

Robert stamped his feet on the doormat and took off his hat as he gingerly entered Dove House. He was keen not to delay the delivery of the words he had come to say. Rather than fulfil the usual formalities of a visit to see the Reverend, he started to speak before they had even sat down. It would have been courteous to ask Cole to sit for such a message but as a man accustomed to living on the island, such considerations were a little foreign to Robert. Living on Sable Island came with a prerequisite for plain-talking, short and straight to the point.

"Cole," he began, as he turned to fully face the priest "I have some bad news concerning Nancy."

"Nancy?" Cole asked. He was suddenly muddled; surely his daughter was elsewhere in the house? Had he been so engrossed in his tasks that he had not even broken bread with his child? He glanced at his pocket watch; it was a little after seven thirty in the evening.

"My, is that really the time? Nancy! She will be in her room reading. Wait, I will go and fetch her." Cole knew that Nancy was often prone to be so engrossed in a book that she would, like him with his sermon preparations, lose all sense of time. Lost in the narrative of a good read.

"No, Cole, you need to hear this," Robert said, looking Cole Haas in the eye as he placed both hands firmly on the reverend's slight shoulders.

"I'm afraid I am the bearer of very bad news, Cole. You must listen to me." His voice was wavering as he struggled to control his own emotions. As a father himself, he knew his words would be as an axe, cutting at the very heart of this poor man before him.

"Cole, Nancy is gone."

"No, Robert, she is just upstairs." Cole broke free from Robert's grasp and headed for Nancy's room.

"Please sit down, my friend. A terrible thing has happened. Nancy is dead." There it was. The words had left Robert James.

Cole hesitated at the foot of the stairs. "No. No, no, Robert you are quite wrong! My daughter is upstairs, I am telling you." Robert could see tears welling in Cole's eyes as the awful truth started to sink in.

"She is dead, my friend," Robert said, in the most sympathetic tone he could muster.

Cole fell to his knees, his hands clutching his face as he started to rock, gently.

"No father should have to bury his own child. That just isn't right. Who is this God that I am supposed to believe in? Robert, what have I done to bring this upon myself?" Cole began to moan. He was unable to get up and Robert stooped down to try and comfort his friend.

He had suffered more grief than one man should expect to fill a lifetime. He had only just come to terms with the loss of his beloved Sophia, and now her legacy, the daughter who reminded him on a daily basis of his late wife, was gone.

Even God would not be able to take away his grief. The grief of Cole Haas would last for the rest of his life.

He had been born in Halifax in 1822. His family, although not religious by practice, were of the old-fashioned values variety, common in Halifax society at the time. The city was evolving from its modest trading roots and establishing itself as the gateway to Europe. There had been, however, a great influx of settlers during the time that Cole grew from baby to boy arriving to seek out possible employment.

His mother was a very stern-looking woman with more than her fair share of facial whiskers. She had a most peculiar voice, a Germanic-Canadian mix. The timbre of her accent echoed throughout the neighbourhood as she bellowed after the whereabouts of her offspring. She had six children, of whom Cole was the youngest. He was often forgotten about and very much left to his own devices. During his childhood, Cole developed reliance on his own company and would often talk to himself. His siblings thought him strange.

Cole was still only a child when he first visited St Peter's Catholic Church on Barrington Street, very close to where he lived. His family rarely noticed his absence and so he often spent time sitting alone in the pews. The Right Reverend William Fraser certainly noticed the young Cole though. The Rev. Fraser would sit alongside Cole when the church was otherwise unoccupied. They made quite a couple; the old religious stalwart and the boy, sitting in St

Peter's as they discussed all sorts of matters. Fraser was a muscular Christian, one who played hockey on Saturdays and preached on Sundays.

Young Cole confided in Fraser, sharing all the things a boy at such an impressionable time felt to be important. The two cemented a friendship over orange segments and cheese sandwiches, a companionship that lasted for many years. The older man's attempts at luring Cole to play hockey, however, were never successful.

St Peter's could not accommodate the growing congregation and, on the back of substantial funds presented to the church by the large Irish contingent in the area, as well as generous donations from local Indian chiefs, it was decided to build an altogether more grandiose place of worship. The new basilica was named St Mary's, and had, at that time, the tallest free-standing granite spire in the world. Shipwrights were hired to construct the roof as they were deemed to have the experience to take on such an ambitious project. In fact, the roof resembled the hull of a boat. Young Cole grew fascinated by the evolving Church and, unbeknownst to his family, started to study the Catholic faith.

Young Cole attended church regularly and, through his friendship to Fraser, became indoctrinated as a Catholic. It was a great surprise to his mother and father when William Fraser – who had recently been appointed bishop – told them their youngest son was to be ordained as a Catholic minister. But who were they to question such an eminent man?

Cole Haas grew into a serious young fellow, who studied hard and was incredibly devout. At the age of twenty-two he was given his first posting as a junior minister. As such, he continued to look to Bishop Fraser, as any young priest would, for spiritual guidance concerning his path to God.

It was during one of his first services that his eyes met those of the gregarious Sophia. She sat on the front pew, her eyes so full of life, and focused on the nervous young reverend. Her parents, sat alongside her, looked agitated as Cole stumbled through his words. They were of the religious old school and did not believe such a young man should be in charge of their weekly sermons. As for himself, Cole tried very hard, too hard perhaps, as he looked down on the scowling faces of the older members of his congregation. Who was he to guide them spiritually? Sophia, however, thought his discomfort very sweet and at the end of the service wanted to talk to Cole.

His brow was covered in sweat as she, with family chaperoning, approached the budding priest.

"Do you believe that all men are born with love in their hearts and only after living life are turned toward darkness?" Sophia asked.

Cole was taken aback. In his formative years, he had not had a great deal of experience in dialogue with young women and frankly did not know how to correctly respond to Sophia. He suddenly noticed how beautiful Sophia was. She had the most gorgeous almond-shaped face; her eyes seemed to burn through him as she maintained a fixed stare on the young minister. His skin began to feel prickly, as he awkwardly shifted from one foot to the other. Nervously brushing his clean-shaven chin with the back of his hand, he considered what would be the appropriate response. He did not want to disappoint this beautiful young woman.

Sophia and her parents dutifully stood, not moving, awaiting his answer. Cole presumed, correctly, that her parents were used to her directness, as they stood like two centurions either side of their confident daughter.

"Well," Cole started, "I think that every one of us has a choice about how we live our lives. God makes it clear that we should walk the path of righteousness and respect our fellow man. I believe that we are all capable of falling off that road. Are we influenced by hardships or turmoil along the way? I would say yes, but still, we have a choice, and maybe spiritual guidance can play a part. Do you think we are all born good and potentially stray due to life experience? I am sorry, I don't know your name."

"Sophia, Sophia Yung. And this is my father, John, and mother, Sarah." Sophia pointed in turn to her parents, who stood silently beside her. "Are those your words or what you have been told by your superiors?"

"Sophia, stop that," Sarah Yung said, with a little embarrassment at her daughter's abruptness.

Cole blushed. She was clearly testing him and yet he took no offence at her questions. Rather, he felt a fluttering in his chest as the young woman before him smiled. Her green eyes were full of mischief and Cole realised she was just teasing him. He liked that.

Within three months they were courting and within six they were married, much to the satisfaction of the church and the Yung family. Everyone who knew them considered them to be a perfect match. A glorious couple that signified all that was right, both physically and spiritually.

As with a lot of the younger members of the Catholic Church, the newlywed Haases embarked on a journey that took them to many places to deliver the message of faith. Sophia welcomed every move. She embraced it with so much enthusiasm that she became pivotal to her husband's early success. She was her husband's rock, firmly supporting his rapid rise through the ranks. Many church elders considered that without Sophia, Cole Haas would have had to settle for limited expectations. They saw the two as one package, one vessel to portray a positive image for the Catholic Church. Cole was fully aware of the importance of his wife's role in his professional life, another facet that only enhanced his deep love for her.

Since her untimely death, he had led his life on automatic. Only the obligation to raise Nancy, as an extension of Sophia, had given him purpose. Church activities were fulfilled in a perfunctory manner, unlike before, when enthusiasm dripped from his every pore. Without his girls there would be nothing. Only the spectre of his complete loss of faith would remain.

So now, as he kneeled, helpless, on the floor, Cole Haas

was a man at a crossroads. He could not call on the spiritual guidance or considerable empathy of Father Fraser, who had passed away two years ago. In terms of faith, Cole was alone with God as his only companion, one that he now resented.

It was questionable whether the loss of both his wife and daughter would lead the Reverend Haas to the darkness he had always feared. Perhaps his loss of faith would be temporary? Either way, he was in a terrible state.

Robert James stood, looking down on poor Cole Haas, who was gently sobbing. He didn't know what to say to this man, his friend who had now lost everything. He was concerned that if he left, Cole would do something stupid. He felt awkward. How should he handle matters?

"Do you wish me to stay with you tonight, Cole?" No reply. "Cole, can you hear me?"

"I must go to Nancy, she needs me. Where is she, Robert? I can't stay here." The reverend said with a sudden clarity.

"I'm not sure that would be a good idea, Cole. It would be best to wait until Tom has cleaned up a bit." He regretted his words instantly, though it was of little importance; Cole barely seemed to notice his exact choice of words.

"What has Tom Madder got to do with Nancy?"

"It's at Tom's house where it happened."

"What happened?"

"Where Nancy was killed, Cole."

"What do you mean, killed?"

"I am so sorry. Nancy was murdered." His words hung

in the air, sharp and detached like an arrow to the heart.

The revelation hit Cole like a thunderbolt. If knowing his daughter was dead was not enough, to think of Nancy as a victim was horrific. "What do you mean?"

"Your Nancy had her life taken, Cole. She was found on the floor in Jacob Madder's bedroom. I am so sorry, my friend."

"I presumed when you said she was dead she had suffered an accident or fallen into the sea. You now tell me someone killed her? Who, and how?"

"They are saying it was Jacob Madder. He has gone on the run and Tom has set off to find him, then hand him to the constable in Lunenburg."

"No, that's wrong, Jacob and Nancy are good friends. They grew up together, he would never hurt my Nancy." As Cole spoke, Robert noticed that he seemed more alert, as if digesting the new information had focused his mind. There would be anger next.

"I have said too much already. I will stay here tonight, then tomorrow we can go to Madder's house."

"I won't believe Jacob has harmed my girl, he's a nice boy and I cannot accept it. I want to go to see her now!"

"It's late, Cole."

"What do you mean, 'late'? You come here, tell me my daughter is dead – no, murdered – and then say it's too late to go and see her? I will not have that. We are going to Madder's house tonight."

"We can't go to Tom's house tonight, he is out on South

Shore trying to find Jacob. Besides, there is something I must tell you. I know this is a bad time but I have to tell you – I should have confided in someone before, but I carry a burden, Cole, and I must tell you."

Robert felt bad. How selfish to put his own needs first on tonight of all nights. He had no idea what to expect from this broken man, yet continued. "Eighteen years ago I found myself near Mahone Bay, in the woods just off of Oak Island. I happened upon a couple's small house, just away from the main trail. I was lost and looking for shelter for the night. The man of the house had left for Truro on an errand or some such thing. I struggle to recall exactly why. The woman was alone. She was very pretty, Cole, a thing of beauty." He paused to collect his thoughts as Cole looked on, barely paying attention.

"The thing is, I had been having a bad time with my Lisbeth. She can be difficult. You know that, don't you? It was she who had sent me there in the first place, on some stupid task. I was too busy with the lighthouse and should not have been on the mainland. I was weak, a weak man, and she was lovely, kind to me, spoke softly. I fucked her – sorry, Cole." He was ashamed at the coarseness of his language. "I mean we made love. I couldn't get her out of my mind for months. I would travel to Oak Island and just watch her. Her husband was a fool. He didn't know how lucky he was to have her, but for some reason she wouldn't leave his side. I spoke only once to her, six months later, when she was expecting and I knew, I really knew, Cole, that child was mine. But she would have nothing to do with me. I begged her to run away with me but she was too good a woman to go on the run with me, she would have been ashamed. I wanted to tell someone, but if my Lisbeth found out she would have me done away with. That's why I can only tell you, Cole, as what's between us stays between us and the Lord Almighty." He sat back and looked at Cole for the first time. The reverend's eyes were glazed over. He had not listened to the story so had no advice to dole out. Cole just sat in silence, his ears tuned out of earthly matters. All he could hear was his own voice asking, "Why, God, why?"

8

Riggins

"PULL THAT LINE OR WE ARE doomed," Tom Madder yelled at his son.

Jacob could see his father was mouthing words, but they were lost in the mayhem of the storm that had hit the small craft. The two men were sailing a route which hugged the eastern coast of Nova Scotia. There had been no evidence of the cyclone when they had pushed away from Sable at dawn. Tom knew that it was best that they keep close to the shore all the way to Halifax, being inexperienced sailors. In his mind, it was simple; 'Get my son off the island before I have to face the shame of questions about Nancy Haas's death'.

Take the safest, quickest route. That was his plan.

Looking down at his hands, Jacob saw that the rope holding the sail in place was slipping from his grasp. Blood and a watery excretion had begun to seep from the blisters that covered his palms. His were hands unaccustomed to salt water and toil; his were hands heavy with the burden of Nancy's death.

The dory was rolling violently in the maelstrom that

was upon them. Tom was on the edge; he needed his son to work in unison to ensure their safety. The wind was so strong that anything that was not tied down in the boat was blown overboard. All that remained was the large wooden trunk that Jacob sat upon. Fear was etched onto his face.

Tom knew they needed help, as he tried to set a course for the shelter within St Margaret's Bay. That was still two miles away and hope was slowly draining from the big man.

They were stuck in the sweep of the storm, which had gathered momentum as it hit the nor'easter front travelling from the west.

"Jesus Christ, boy, do you want to die?" Tom was rapidly losing faith in his own ability to steer them to safety. He looked at his small son, who now had a green pallor and, having abandoned the rope controlling the sail, was clinging for dear life to the trunk.

Jacob was transfixed by the dark swirl that surrounded the dory; they seemed small and insignificant against the vast expanse of the sea. The sky above them was angry; darkness splattered with falling drops of icy water.

The boom that held the sail was loose and swinging from side to side. Tom had to stay aware of the spruce pole, as any wrong move would lead to being struck by it. He was trying to balance the boat by widening his stance and was now in a precarious position at the bow of the boat. He knew that he had to get to the mid–point, as his son, who was virtually a dead weight, had let go of both rope and rudder. The boat was now at the mercy of the elements.

Without warning, the wind seemed to abate, the surface of the water becoming smooth, as if oil had been poured around them. Jacob sat up as Tom looked beyond the transom of the boat, his face momentarily frozen, eyes unblinking. Jacob had never seen such a look on any man's face. In an instant, his father was pushing towards the tiller, snagging his trouser on the eye that held the oars in place. Jacob followed his father's look to see a great funnel just thirty feet from the boat.

The wind returned with a vengeance, howling in a vortex that engulfed the vessel. They were surely doomed. Tom knew he had to act fast or they and the dory would be sucked under. He needed to both balance the boat and steer her in a way that would mean they were spat out to safer water by the great tube of rushing air.

Tom Madder reached out to grab the tiller that moved violently from one side of the transom to the other.

"I can't make it!" he cried, as he straightened his back to maximise his reach. The spruce spar that had been swinging from side to side hit his head so hard that it knocked him off his feet. He lay motionless in the boat, blood flowing from a large gash on his temple. He was unconscious.

"Father!" Jacob screamed.

The boat was now spinning at great speed. Jacob was so dizzy he lost his bearings and staggered about. The combination of his inability as a mariner and his sheer panic added to his confusion.

He sat down on the trunk, looking at his father lying

static on the floor of the boat. He presumed him dead. Grasping his hands together, he prayed.

"Dear Lord, I am sorry for the things I have done. Please save my father's soul and spare me. If you do this I promise to make things right, or else I give up and you should take me now to spend eternity as you see fit."

The trunk shifted. Unknown to Jacob, one of the stiff leather bindings had worked free and was now flapping loosely. Like a large snake, it coiled round Jacob's slender calf, trapping the boy against the body of the trunk.

The dory pitched violently as it spun out of control. Jacob and the trunk were thrown forward as one, projected into air so damp it seemed at one with the ocean. The strange package was sucked up into the epicentre of the twister, rising to a great height, spinning and spinning. Jacob was in a trance. He seemed unaware of the trunk still strapped to his leg.

The great storm spat them out and they sailed through the air, falling amongst the waves. They were submerged at once. Jacob, eyes fully open, looked straight ahead through the water, as the spinning slowly decreased. The saltwater aggravated his cornea He felt strangely at peace, submerged in the unnatural environment.

Like a cork escaping from a bottle, the trunk returned to the surface, popping out into the raging water. Jacob exhaled sharply, letting forth a cry. His lungs registered pain, his leg registered pain, his whole body registered pain.

He needed to secure his upper body onto the trunk. With

herculean effort, he slipped his arm through the second strap, which was still secure around the container. His leg, still trapped after such an incredible flight, was numb, his large toe contorted as cramp had set in. Although in a confused state, he knew he had to keep his head above the lapping waters.

He let out a final wild yell, then fell silent, attached to this most unlikely life-raft as it rode the waves.

To the south of the tempest, the dory, battered and broken, plotted a course out to sea. A shaft of weak sunlight burst through the cloud–cover, resulting in a blue–green iridescence forming around the boat. Large flakes of snow drifted against this funnel of light, as if Poseidon himself was gently tossing pieces of paper from beyond the clouds. Inside the dory lay Tom Madder. He was unconscious and had lost a lot of blood. The bloody soup splashed against his bruised body.

In a dream, Tom could see a mermaid. Three seagulls held her above the waves. An iridescent hue surrounded the mythical sea creature as she rose over the swell. In her outstretched hand sat a small red boat, sails aloft as if she had plucked the vessel direct from the sea. The vision faded. His breathing became shallow as the dory moved forward.

Hurricane Saxby Gale had moved inland as quickly as she had hit the seaboard. Her track hit the Bay of Fundy with full force, dissipating one day later. Behind her, the sea was calm, the only evidence of the hurricane being a mass of floating debris gently moving in unison with the tide. Seabirds were yet to return, and so an eerie silence prevailed. A light snow started to float down from the darkened sky.

Riggins and Thomsen had left Lunenburg as soon as the winds abated, aboard the thirty foot long "Myrna Lee". The two were sailing up the coast in search of treasure. They had been told of the money pit at Oak Island; in fact, every sailor worth his salt knew of the pirate treasure hoard. They assumed that, due to the storm, no boat or man would care about two ragged seafarers going about their business.

Thomsen, as always, said nothing. He had not spoken a word for years, through choice rather than affliction. Riggins, however, being accustomed to his shipmate's ways, spoke enough for them both. He held a running commentary on anything and everything.

"Well, Thomsen, we set a good course beyond Mahone Bay and should hit Oak Island by nightfall. Yes, you're right, it will be hard, but we never been afraid of hard work, have we? Bloody won't know we're coming, will they? I heard they shot a man last month for digging. They won't be shooting no-one on this boat, will they, Thomsen?"

Thomsen, an accomplished rower, set a good pace, considering the absence of wind. The boat was packed full with shovels, wooden planks, rope, oyster bags, and explosives. Together, they formed a serious treasure hunter's kit, bound together on the floor of the boat.

Riggins, a rotund and most confrontational individual, stood at an above average sixty-eight inches. He wore a dark red shirt and thick green pants held up by a broad black leather belt. He always carried a short-bladed dagger, tucked into his belt by an ornately-marked sheath. He had acquired the blade from a dead man lying outside the Old Inn in Yarmouth several years before. The dagger had a most unusual curved wooden handle that had once housed several small jewels. The jewels were gone; Riggins presumed correctly that they had been prised out of the wood in order to pay debts the deceased previous owner had run up. Riggins hoped one day to replace the jewels.

His long dark hair, slicked back by lard, was tied in a ponytail by an old scarf given to him by a prostitute. Her name was Myrna Lee, and he loved her, stupidly assuming that she held similar feelings for him. Once he had the Oak Island treasure he could tell Myrna that she should change profession and live with the burly sailor full-time. This would, in truth, be a great surprise to the busty wench. A surprise which would not overly welcome to the professional lady.

Riggins' right leg, being much larger than his left, hampered him, and led him to favour one side as he walked. Thomsen imagined that if Riggins walked forward he would complete a full circle within the hour. This thought amused the silent sailor.

Riggins was also known to like a drink and was constantly inebriated. He emitted the sweet whiff of liquor and this, mixed with his body odour, led to a pungent aroma surrounding him. It was said you could always tell when Abe Riggins was near.

"Look lively, Thomsen, don't delay." Riggins took a large swig of golden nectar from his trusty little brown jug. He did not offer any sustenance to his companion. Thomsen rowed, Riggins was in charge.

Sweat was rolling from Thomsen's forehead and his fleshy cheeks were sucked in due to the constant slog, giving him a rather slippery appearance. Flakes of snow started to accumulate on his thick mop of hair, giving him a white lustre.

Up ahead, off to the port side on the horizon, a large wooden trunk was swaying with the gentle movement of the tide. A small boy was strapped to the trunk. He looked as if he were sleeping peacefully, but as he was on the opposite side of the trunk, he could not be seen by the two-man crew of the Myrna Lee.

"Thomsen, what have we here? This could be our lucky day, my friend. Aim for that beautiful discovery, who knows what could be inside? This indeed is a fine day for treasuring."

The boat turned thirty degrees, and headed for Jacob and the trunk.

9

The Broken Shoe

1857

TWELVE YEARS AGO ON A SUNNY September morning the local fishermen paused from their duties to see who was arriving. As was always the case the arrival of the horse-drawn carriage was met with a certain curiosity.

"Lunenburg, next stop is Lunenburg." The stagecoach had taken twelve arduous hours to make the journey from Halifax. The ride had been brutal. Four large horses steamed a milky sweat; they had pulled the coach for the last twenty-six miles at a decent pace.

Four guards – members of the military – sat atop a carriage that had six passengers inside. Various luggage items were tethered to the back of the main carriage. It was a wonder that none had fallen off during the bumpy journey.

The driver, dusty and damp, stepped down and brushed off the dirt that had accumulated on his thick leather coat.

Reverend Cole Haas, his wife Sophia, and their young

daughter, Nancy, alighted from the coach. They were overjoyed to finally be disembarking from the equine-driven vehicle. For a moment, Cole Haas felt his body continue to vibrate, his ears struggling to make sense of his daughter's questions.

Sophia, being a practical wife, thanked the driver and took in her new surroundings. This was to be their home. To her right was the main dock, to her left, steep stone steps ascended between various buildings. She counted at least five passages climbing from the harbour to what she presumed was the main town of Lunenburg. She also noted an unusually shaped rock, complete with inscription, at the foot of the steps closest to her.

"Mummy, look."

Her attention shifted like any mother's would at the sound of her own child. Sophia's eyes followed her daughter's slender arm, outstretched and pointing directly at a great barrel of fish seemingly abandoned on the main road.

How strange, Sophia thought.

"Come on Nancypants, let's find our new house. Then we may be able to have some cake." She knew how to cajole her daughter, and the promise of cake did the trick.

"Come on, Papa, let's go up the mountain!"

Cole was also looking at the scale of the path to their new home, and then down at the four cases containing some of their most important possessions. 'Good Lord, I will need help with this,' he thought. He was glad that the stagecoach company had set restrictions over baggage allowed on the actual journey. Most of the family's belongings would follow in a few days.

The family had arrived in the fall of 1857. The Reverend Haas was to take up his post as the resident preacher at St Norbert's Roman Catholic Church on York Street, Lunenburg. The church had been completed in 1839 and was designed to make a statement, as the only Roman Catholic place of worship in the province.

Built in the Georgian ecclesiastical style, the church was unmistakably gothic. The towering steeple was reminiscent of a witch's hat and many folk would visit the church just to peer at this most unusual style of roof.

Any early enthusiasm for attendance had waned in recent times. Worshippers were simply failing to turn up, and it was hoped that having a younger, passionate priest would reverse this situation.

Previous incumbents at St Norbert's were responsible for vast areas, including the many islands prevalent around South Shore. But travelling by pony and trap cut into time that would be better served spreading the Catholic message to a somewhat sceptical population. Besides, the majority of mariners were put off by the pietistic nature of the other churches in the area, particularly the Lutherans. It was a competitive market, so to speak, and St Norbert's needed an increase in worshippers.

Sophia Haas looked up on that crisp morning at her husband's new place of work and expressed pure delight at the shape of the steeple. She possessed a wonderfully contagious laugh, and this, coupled with her preternaturally warm disposition, ensured an instant popularity among local residents.

The family Haas, during their time at St Norbert's, lived in one of the small cape-styled houses on Montague Street. Originally built in 1753 by the first settlers to Lunenburg, the home was modest, considered quaint.

Playing cards, upon which surnames were written, were chosen at random to allocate the building plots in what is now the main town area of which Montague Street forms a part. In 1749, almost three thousand immigrants had arrived at the port of Halifax – the state capital – from the Upper Rhine region. As part of their passage they were then required to work on various projects – mostly military-based – before being able to spread across the province.

Eight hundred families travelled the seventy miles south from the capital, to arrive on the coast just to the north of the La Have River. The native Indians had named the appellation "Malllggaet", meaning white foaming billows, in reference to the Atlantic surf.

Upon arrival, the newcomers renamed the place Lunenburg, after Litenburg in Northern Germany – their homeland. The name was chosen as a constant reminder of the country these adventurers had said goodbye to.

One hundred years later, Sophia Haas was to live, albeit only briefly, in a place where locals considered themselves doubly-blessed. "Contented lives – contented dies," they would say to any visitor who demonstrated any interest whatsoever in their town.

Reverend Haas was certainly not contented given the tragic circumstances of his wife's premature demise.

It was a fine summer morning when Sophie Haas woke for what was to be her final day on Earth. She was happy and settled. Her daughter, Nancy, now aged nine, was the primary cause of her wellbeing. She was contented. Contented lives.

She prepared the breakfast as she did every morning; it was six-thirty and she paused to enjoy the quietness of the house. Her kitchen was very small but Sophia had nevertheless arranged the various cooking implements so that she could prepare any meal with an economy of effort. She knew her husband and young daughter would wake at any moment and the normalities of daily life would resume. Routine was something that Sophia enjoyed. It was a consequence of being an ambitious reverend's wife that they had spent much of their married life moving from one town to another. She was hopeful that Lunenburg would be home for many years to come.

A creak on the old wooden staircase announced the arrival of her husband. The smell of home-baked oatmeal bread had alerted his senses. It was time to get up. Dappled sunlight filled the kitchen as Cole approached his wife, who was busy stirring some hot milk in a copper pan. He wrapped his arms around her slender waist.

"Good morning, my love. Breakfast smells good."

"Is Nancy awake yet?"

"No, I swear that girl would sleep through a storm! Can I help with anything?"

"Sit yourself at the table, dear. I will go and get Nancy."

Sophia Haas was the perfect wife and as she left the room, Cole sat back, feeling contented. He was a lucky man.

After breakfast, Cole had gone to see Miss Zwicker on a church-related matter. The old spinster was a powerful figure in Lunenburg's religious circle. When she announced she needed to speak to the Reverend, he responded with urgency. Nancy had been walked to school just five minutes away, Miss Gow's private school on Prince St., Lunenburg.

Miss Gow ran her small school in two rooms, rented in a building owned by the Presbyterian Church. The church discouraged attendance from children of other faiths, yet Miss Gow was an educator first and last and she would not refuse any child entry to her classroom. "Church rules stay outside my school. I pay the rent, I decide which children I teach," the ardent Miss Gow would say.

Sophia had the rest of the day to herself. She had been "Volunteered", as Cole put it, to represent him on a number of local committees. Dutifully, she would attend these meetings. However, today was her own and she was free of any commitments.

The front door slammed shut as Sophia headed south to browse the small shops of Main Street. She was wearing a striking blue dress and a navy shawl. Her boots were old, soft leather, with well-worn soles from constant use. Sophia had glued the right boot heel – which had broken off – in place as a temporary repair; Cole had pressed her for weeks to get the boots professionally repaired.

Sophia was always frugal, especially with her own possessions. She would rather save her allowance for the more precious things. Today she intended to buy Nancy a pewter broach as a keepsake. She had seen the sand dollar design in the window of Young & Sons. The merchants had made a name manufacturing whale oil lamps in pewter but due to a decline in demand for more practical lines they had begun to make more decorative items.

Sand dollars held a special place in Sophia's heart. Her late mother had taken her on many summer trips to search the beaches of Atlantic Canada for the delicate, burrowing sea urchins. As a girl, she had owned a large collection, keeping them in a special box. She dated each one discovered and, in recent times, had often shown them to Nancy. She would tell stories of how and when she had found each dollar. Nancy loved them.

Stuffing the newly-purchased broach deep into her pocket, Sophia left Young & Sons and decided to walk down to the dockside to take in the ocean. Those who lived and worked so close to such a great body of water know that you develop an affinity for the ocean. Sophia loved to stand by the main dock and breathe in the salty air. It invigorated her.

Leaving Main Street, she headed down one of the steep paths leading to the main dock. Like a young child, she skipped the first few steps. Upon reaching the fifth step she had gained quite a pace and as she descended she started to sing. A happy song it was.

As she planted her right boot on the next step the heel gave way, spinning off in a shallow arc, lost in the overgrown verge. Sophia felt a sharp pain as her ankle bore the full weight of her descent. An audible rip was heard as her ankle ligament snapped. She was now rolling head over heels like a ball, gathering more speed as she careered down the remaining steps.

Sophia Haas did not feel additional pain from the final blow to her head. She hit the commemorative stone so hard that she was instantly killed. Her warm blood trickled between the letters carved in the grey stone, congealing in the wells of the carved indentations naming Lunenburg's sailors lost at sea.

Cole Haas had now lost his pretty young wife and was raising his daughter Nancy alone. He was struggling with his faith. Losing a loved one under horrific circumstances can do that to any man. The question of God's great intention was now a constant source of misery to the reverend, as he wrestled with his beliefs.

Sermons at St Norbert's became darker; other communications with his parishioners became abrupt. The reverend was considered a social pariah. Churchgoers, and even those who had never set foot in a place of worship, would go out of their way not to run into the reverend Haas.

"Quick, cross the road, Haas is nearly upon us," the townsfolk would unfairly say.

After two years of his very public mourning, his superiors thought it would be a good idea for the young preacher and his daughter to have a fresh start and spread the Catholic word to the inhabitants of Sable Island.

10

The Money Pit

THE MYRNA LEE GLIDED SILENTLY THROUGH the water as she approached the bobbing trunk. Thomsen expertly pulled alongside the floating wooden chest with one final tug of an oar. Fortunately, the sea was calm and the winds had remained light, as Riggins reached over, attempting to lift the box onto their boat.

"Come and help bring this beauty aboard, Mr Thomsen. I can't lift it by myself."

Raising his right arm, Riggins stretched out to grab the far side of the trunk. As he searched for a good grip his hand found the smooth, limp hand of Jacob Madder. The touch was icy cold. A modest covering of snow had not melted and, despite the occasional splashing of salt water, was clinging to any part of Jacob that was exposed above sea level. The chill touch made Riggins believe that the hand must belong to something unnatural.

"Aaah!" he screamed, quickly snatching his own hand away from the frozen limb. "What is this devilment? I think we have us a mermaid or some peculiar sea creature, Thomsen. I don't want us cursed," Riggins said as he fell back into the boat. He was like a lot of sailors of the time; a superstitious man who believed all the stories and legends passed down from generation to generation. "Done nothing wrong, paid my way and respected the sea, so leave me be," he chanted over and over as he began to furiously form a cross across his thick torso.

Calmly, Thomsen, using one of his oars, pushed the trunk full circle to see the other side. There, strapped to the floating box, was the unconscious boy. Blond hair hung limply from the boy's small head and his clothes were torn and twisted, barely covering his pallid form. In some ways, Jacob Madder did bear the look of something unworldly.

Both men were now standing up in their boat, looking silently at each other.

Riggins had at least stopped chanting and crossing himself. Yet he was a man seldom short of dialogue. His silence only lasted a few seconds.

"Is it dead?" Riggins asked, as he looked at Jacob's pale body, hanging from the two leather straps of the trunk. "Poke it with your oar, Thomsen."

Thomsen, who was reaching out to get a firm grip of the sodden trunk, looked up at Riggins. He was beginning to question the wisdom of his partnership with a man like Abe Riggins. Holding the trunk with one hand, he was now looking at the straps that held the waif in place. He drew his knife, which was held by the scabbard tied to the belt around his waist, and started to cut through the nearest strap. Once released from the first binding, the boy fell backwards into the ocean.

"That's right, Thomsen, cut it loose."

Thomsen was concerned about the boy and looked through the surface of the water to see a serene face looking back at him. Jacob seemed as if he was sleeping peacefully. His blond hair pulsed beneath the water. Thomsen paused, taking time to study the boy's pretty face. Suddenly, eyes opened and were looking back at the silent sailor, who recoiled with shock.

Jacob felt a vice-like pressure in his chest. Seawater and debris that had attached itself during the storm fell from his body as Thomsen reached down and pulled him out. He placed Jacob carefully on the floor of the boat, uncertain about how to revive his charge. The boy looked barely alive. By instinct, he took off his jacket and wrapped Jacob like a parcel, then started to vigorously rub the boy's shoulders.

Although fascinated by Jacob, Riggins was altogether more concerned that the trunk should not be lost. "Thomsen!" he shouted, "The trunk, we need it in the boat! Maybe treasure or valuables lie inside? Look lively, man!"

Thomsen was fairly ignorant about medical procedures for reviving drowning men, although he knew that warmth was key. He was aware that prolonged exposure to the cold Atlantic water could stop the heart of any man, and if this boy were to survive, it would be a miracle.

He came from old fishing stock that believed the sea was a female entity; drowned men belonged to her. He was also led to believe that those rescued from drowning lived on borrowed time and that she would get them in the end. "What the sea wants, the sea gets," his elders had told him.

As he stood, silently observing the boy, he dearly wished that rather than expire there and then in the well of the boat, the boy would wake up. To live on borrowed time, however long that might be. His attachment to the boy was somewhat alien to him; he was only used to being in the company of Riggins – who had no likeable traits. Perhaps the helplessness and the serenity in Jacob's childish face made Thomsen feel such empathy. He reached down as he placed his ear to Jacob's mouth, hoping to feel the breath of life, anything. He didn't realise that he was holding Jacob's hand, gently rubbing across the back of it with his thumb.

Jacob heaved, then started to cough out salty liquid. His wheezing was violent and the two men looked at his pale body, as his lungs demanded air.

"Sit him up, Thomsen, it's just a boy!" Riggins was clearly relieved that the visitor to the Myrna Lee was human after all. "Thomsen, the trunk, let's bring it aboard."

Thomsen placed Jacob against a large, soft bag of coiled rope and set about landing the big box that had saved the boy's life. It took him ten minutes to lift it out of the water. It was so heavy that he wondered how it had remained afloat.

Riggins was immediately working on the clasp, pawing at it. He could hardly contain his excitement as he opened the trunk. Thomsen knew from the look on Riggins's face that disappointment hung in the air above the boat.

"No, no good, rubbish, waste of time," Riggins said,

between tossing various items overboard. A floating catalogue of Tom Madder's possessions lay in a line behind the Myrna Lee. Finally, with a great yell, Riggins tossed the whole trunk into the Atlantic. "Let some other sailor waste their time on this crap."

Thomsen raised his eyebrow, looked squarely at Jacob, who had meanwhile drifted into a dream, and started to gather his oars. He knew what was to happen next, even though he would rather continue to examine Jacob's pale body.

"We have wasted far too much time on this folly. The boy will most certainly not last the day. I'd be surprised if he hasn't got the pneumonia. Let us set sail Thomsen, we need speed. To Oak Island, the money pit, and the treasure!" Riggins declared with surprising glee, given the fruitless nature of their find. Perhaps though, if the boy survived, he could be of considerable use when they reached Oak Island. A plan began to form in his most devious mind.

As they approached the inlet of Oak Island, they were cheered to find that the Saxby Gale had destroyed the strip of earth that normally restricted access to the bay. The man-made barrier had been constructed in 1859 to discourage bounty hunters, who arrived having heard of the possibility of hidden pirate treasure.

Thomsen slowed his stroke rate; the air was so still that as Jacob came round, he could hear the drops of salt water dripping from the wooden oars into the sea. Riggins stood at the bow of the Myrna Lee, rigid, shoulders back, as if trying to be dignified. He was straining to plot a good course now that the light was almost gone. Thankfully, the snow had only fallen in sporadic drifts and the lack of wind ensured that the weather remained settled for now.

"Steady as she goes, Thomsen," he whispered, whilst raising his left arm to signal the course he wanted them to take. "Five degrees to port," he continued. Riggins wore the stare of a possessed man. His voice rasped instructions as he scanned for an appropriate landing spot. They would need to secure the Myrna Lee out of sight in the open bay. The storm had ensured that the Oak Island residents – who were fiercely protective of their claim – were kept busy, and it being so late in the day they were most probably in their various homes, not suspecting that visitors had arrived. Riggins did not wish to warrant unnecessary attention to their pilfering. Many a man had been chased from Oak Island since it had become private property and, in recent times, fiercely guarded by those who laid claim to the one-mile square landmass.

Years before, three teenage boys, having observed mysterious green lights emanating just off Western Shore, felt compelled to investigate. They soon discovered a clear circular indentation in the mix of sand and stone just beyond the tree line. They returned the following day, at dusk with shovels and by dawn had dug deep enough to unearth the money pit. It was 1795. They kept their discovery secret for a number of months, during which time they had managed to dig down over thirty feet. Every ten feet they came across oak planks, strapped together as a platform. They also found coconut husk matting, which was not native to Nova Scotia. The boys could not keep the secret and had told one too many about the strange goings on they had uncovered at Oak Island. Tales and stories began to emerge, mostly untrue, about what lay below the island. Theories about curses guarding the supposed treasure also became commonplace during conversations in local taverns.

The Truro Mining Company took over excavations and, on one of the initial digs, found three links of a gold chain. This heightened expectations, but after several years of exploration, nothing of any real value was unearthed. Nonetheless, the tale of the tiny gold links grew into legend and motivated a new breed of man to arrive to seek his fortune.

With such expectations and mystery, it was no surprise that in the following years the pit had grown to be over ninety feet in depth, as prospectors arrived to search for gold. Two deaths had not discouraged attempts to find potential fame and fortune.

It was claimed that a giant crow sat amongst the trees surrounding the money pit, warding off potential visitors with mocking reverberations that echoed through the branches. Packs of wild dogs with glowing red eyes were also mooted to roam the small island, in search of eager treasure hunters. It is not known if such stories were started to discourage attempts or to perhaps increase the myth surrounding this small, otherwise insignificant plot of land.

"There! That's where we land!" Riggins pointed with his bony finger to a stone-covered beach, close to where the money pit was supposed to be located. Moonlight alone now illuminated their passage.

Thomsen stopped rowing and the boat gently beached. A light crunching sound signalled that the bottom of the boat was scraping land. Riggins leapt from the boat, landing squarely on the grey-pebbled shore. They had arrived!

"Right, Thomsen, there is much work to be done. We best hurry up, so bring those supplies ashore. We need to hide them in the trees. Let the boy carry his share." Riggins strode off the beach, passing quickly into the pine trees that covered most of the island.

Thomsen busily secured the Myrna Lee by tying a rope through the eye of the hook on the bow to the nearest stable tree. He secured the line with a running bowline knot. The Saxby Gale had blown many of the younger trees out to sea and Thomsen had wisely tested the robustness of his chosen tree by rocking it with his full weight. He then began to unload the equipment and place the various items on the stony beach. Jacob wanted to help him, but he was still wary of his travelling companions and decided to observe rather than engage by assisting the clearly put-upon Thomsen. This made him feel guilty. For his part, Thomsen was beginning to harbour ill feelings about the trip. He grew concerned that they were embarking on the quest at the wrong time – in winter. The cold wind and forming ice were no friends; experience told him that dangers lay ahead.

Riggins, hands on hips with legs astride, stood at the edge of the pit. It was clearly marked by the amount of timber stacked high at its circumference. Reaching for his hip flask, he took a substantial slug of the potent contents. The lantern by his feet cast wavy shadows, ghostly mirages that seemed sinister and strange. It irritated him that it was too dark and there would be no explorations until dawn. Opportunity rarely opened its door for men like Riggins and tonight he once again felt that particular door locked and bolted. Leaving the pit ghosts for the night, he returned to check on Thomsen's progress in setting up camp.

Thomsen was crouched next to the fire he had made and was placing a small tin filled with fresh water within the flames. He wanted Jacob to recover. Still wrapped in Thomsen's thick jacket, Jacob sat motionless against a tree stump, trying to absorb the modest warmth given out by the fire.

"Who is you then, young fella?" Riggins asked as he re-tied his ponytail. "You do understand English? Perhaps you be just like Thomsen here, economic with his words. His choice, mind you."

"Jacob, Jacob Madder from Sable Island." Jacob's voice was croaky and faint

"Speak up, lad. See, Thomsen? He understands me." Riggins seemed secretly pleased that the possibility existed that he may have someone to actually talk to. Maybe, just maybe, his words would summon a response from this nymph torn from the sea.

"Have I told you about how I acquired the Myrna Lee, Jacob Madder? Oh, and the real Myrna, she is one hell of a woman, that she is," Riggins continued, between large glugs from his trusty flask.

Jacob was extremely tired and every part of his body ached. He closed his eyes as Riggins prattled on about being in the Salt Tavern in February 1864 and coming across the busty lady of ill-repute. Jacob was soon asleep, but this did not deter Riggins, who carried on with his well-worked story regardless of having no audience.

Thomsen, who was resting against the stump of a broken tree, turned away. He had heard this tale one hundred times and couldn't bear to listen to Riggins talking about his favourite prostitute and his old boat named in her somewhat dubious honour. He pretended to be asleep.

Who knew what tomorrow would bring? Eventually, Riggins and his unlikely comrades were all asleep. The day spent sailing from Lunenburg had taken its toll. Jacob waited for a dream ghost to arrive, his body still swaying with an imaginary swell even though he was now on dry land. Underneath the blanket that Thomsen had placed over him, Jacob rubbed his thumb across the tops of his fingers. They still bore thick ridges from being partly submerged for so long. He wondered if they would ever flatten out? Meanwhile, Riggins dreamed of treasure and

Thomsen dared to imagine life without his vulgar partner.

Back out on the open ocean, a dory floated, seemingly at the will of wind and tide. No sail was attached to the broken mast, no rudder attached to the damaged transom, no fisherman on board, or so it seemed. Inside, on the floor at the bow, lay a man, motionless in a slush of seawater and blood. Movement; whitish bubbles emerged from Tom Madder's mouth. He retched, coughing uncontrollably. He felt pain. So much pain that for a moment he forgot that his son had been catapulted into the abyss. He moved onto one side, so that his face was fully out of the bloody soup sloshing about in the bottom of the boat. The gash on his face was now out of the water and weeping, left to the mercy of the winter weather, which was unseasonably still. Light winds and drifting snowflakes heralded the onset of a colder spell yet to come. He closed his eyes and returned to his torpor, sensing only the distant cry of seabirds.

11

Darkness

"LOWER JACOB DOWN, MR THOMSEN," RIGGINS bellowed, giving his colleague the simple instruction. He was eager to find out what lay deep below the rocky surface of Oak Island.

Jacob was very frightened as he looked up to see the circle of light fade above him, as if he were looking the wrong way through a ship's telescope. The damp stench of rotting vegetation filled his nostrils, and darkness enveloped the young boy as he descended into the abyss. The rope juddered as Thomsen adjusted his grip. Jacob only weighed ninety-six pounds yet as he dangled in the mouth of the great pit, Thomsen struggled, lactic acid filling his muscles as the slow burn of a cramp grew in his biceps. Riggins, naturally, did not help.

Jacob felt cold his only light being a small lantern crudely attached to the rope just above his head. It cast unusual shadows against the wall of the pit, and the unevenness caused by crude drilling and digging techniques made Jacob think this was a journey to Hell itself. The walls seemed alive, as if they were giant earthworms writhing to get away from his shimmering lantern.

He passed three broken platforms, each made from oak planks loosely bound together by what appeared to be vines. Previous explorers had obviously hacked away at these planks upon reaching them. It must have taken great effort to burst through the solid wood here in the gloom. The planks had presumably been put in place by whoever had constructed the hole in the first place. It occurred to Jacob that these stages were of little use to anybody who was lowered into this place. Why, then, were they here?

In the semi-darkness, Jacob started to think about Nancy. It was so quiet in the depths that he became aware of the sound of his own blood coursing through his body. He desperately wanted to remember what had happened on that fateful day. Was he solely responsible for her demise? There must have been more to it. His thoughts moved onto his father, who was by now surely dead. As Jacob had been catapulted into the eye of the Saxby Gale, the last view he had had of his dory was looking down on his father, lying as if asleep during an ordinary fishing trip. Jacob had lost sight of the boat as he and the trunk had twisted away, and he'd lost consciousness.

His lifeline jolted to a stop, and far above him, he could hear Riggins barking out instructions to the hapless Thomsen.

"Use a sheet bend – no, a rolling hitch would be better. How deep can we go?" Riggins spewed in rapid succession. They were running out of rope.

Deep below, Jacob was left suspended in mid-air. The next platform was eight feet away and the splintered ledge was not large enough to break his fall. He grew concerned that the rope would snap at any moment. His worries weren't helped by the sound of the damp rope creaking loudly, as it swung back and forth. Gusts of air emanated from the well of the pit, whistling past him in waves. A dank odour engulfed him as one of the gusts blew out his lantern. It was completely dark.

Thomsen was trying to tie their final coil of rope to the line that Jacob was held on. He used a rolling hitch knot, which he could tie with one hand. He had wrapped the end of the main line around his waist and was leaning all his weight back to stop Jacob from being swung about within the pit. Riggins was scratching his oily head and muttering to himself. "That will be nearly one hundred feet of rope. How deep can this thing be?"

Jacob was trying to understand what destiny could have possibly led him to this sticky end. To die deep within the earth, left for the worms and mud creatures to devour, was surely not his pre-determined lot. With light there is always hope, but darkness quells a man's spirit. Jacob was about to give up, to untie himself from the slender piece of timber that he sat upon, to launch himself into the abyss and join his mother, father, and Nancy in eternity.

For some unknown reason though, he drove his hand into his trouser pocket to find a small tin box. How strange, he thought. In the darkness, he felt for the smooth edges opposite a small hinge. Inside the box his small fingers felt four tiny sticks of wood – matches! Thomsen had placed them there without his knowledge, whilst he was focused on the task Riggins had ordered him to do. Would light renew his spirit?

The first match sparked, yet failed to ignite. Same with the second, and soon hope was fading once more. He waited until his face felt a rush of air, and struck the third match. A deep yellow flash gave way to the orange glow of flame. Quickly, yet careful not to extinguish the match, he lit the lantern just above his head. He was breathing more heavily as a result of holding his breath whilst he lit the lamp.

Looking below his feet, he could just make out the next layer of oak beams with their familiar broken edges. He strained his eyes to make out what lay beyond this particular platform, but was unable to see, given the poor light this far down.

Looking next at the walls of the pit, he could see various roots protruding out, presumably from the pine trees way above his head. He reached out to grip one of the more slender stems, and, as he gained a grip, was able to pull himself toward the side of the hole. Everywhere felt cold and damp, yet as he pulled at the rope-like root, he was amazed by the strength of just one small tentacle. Once he had regained his composure, he was able to let go, swinging from side to side. Above ground, he would have enjoyed the experience, but deep in the mineshaft he felt apprehension.

It was an alien place, filled with subterranean secrets.

Up above, Riggins was peering down as the rope creaked from side to side at the mouth of the pit. He shouted at Jacob, "What are you playing at boy? Do you want to pull Thomsen down there?"

Jacob looked up. He could barely make out the shape of Riggins, only noticing an indentation in the otherwise perfect circle of light, like the partial eclipse of a full moon. He tore away a dry part of his shirt and wrapped it around the thin root he had ripped from the wall. Placing this hastily constructed torch on his lap, he opened Thomsen's tin and pulled out the last match. Knowing he only had one shot at lighting the torch, he took his time. A clear rasp and the match exploded into life. Dropping the tin, he held the flame in one hand and picked up the torch in the other. Bringing the match to the torn material, he prayed. At first the flamed dulled. Then followed a drift of smoke and, finally, the torch was alight. He knew he didn't have a lot of time, as he wafted the torch in all directions. The pit seemed alive and he could now clearly see where previous visitors had hacked away at the oak platforms above and below. Unfortunately, with the light cast from his makeshift torch being so dim, he could not make out what lay beyond his feet.

The rope juddered and he was lowered another foot. Pausing, he looked up, but could not see or hear the men at the surface. The torch was beginning to burn so rapidly that he now had to make a decision. He needed to know what lay below; how far would he fall? In that moment, he held the torch out towards the centre of the pit and released it.

The torch fell, flames cascading like a shooting star in the darkness. It landed with a hiss, barely ten feet from where Jacob hung. The bottom of this great hole was within a short distance. For a brief moment, Jacob took in as much as he could, then the light was gone. He had not noticed the movement of the rodents scurrying away from the intrusion. He had, however, noticed the coir matting that lay on the floor of the money pit.

Above ground, Thomsen had finally secured the last coil of rope, and was ready to continue lowering Jacob further into the pit. But within moments, the rope went limp. His first thought was that Jacob had fallen off the seat.

Jacob had arrived at the bottom of the pit. His only light was the small lantern attached to the rope. The flame started to fade, as the wick had burned away. Darkness enveloped Jacob like a shroud.

"Madder," Riggins cried out. "What are you playing at? I remind you I need to know what lies down there." His voice echoed in the dark, failing to reach Jacob's ears, as he lay in the gloom at the bottom of the pit. "Madder, you little shit, answer me!"

Jacob could hear noises. Faint voices from above, words he could not decipher. And also scratching sounds originating from below, just beyond the main excavation. What could be hidden so far below ground? What monster now shared its home with Jacob Madder?

12

Island Whispers

"I KNEW HE WAS A BAD lad from the moment I laid eyes on him. He comes from poor stock. With a father like his it is no wonder that he went wayward. What he needed was a mother's touch. All hope for him was lost when Laura met her maker," Irene Beck said with certainty. Mrs Beck had white hair and a furrowed, weather-beaten face, yet young, alert eyes. She was typical of women that lived on Sable; fiercely protective of her husband, Franck, and sceptical of anyone and everyone else. She had a lipless mouth and as her husband sat listening to her, he noticed no movement of her face as she spoke. It was strange that in over twenty years of marriage he had not noticed this fact. Perhaps he had never looked properly at Mrs Irene Beck.

"No, Irene. Jacob was – sorry – is not a bad boy. Just confused, like a lot of youngsters these days. You're right though, the boy misses his mother," Franck replied as he sat rubbing his bad leg, which felt worse than ever. Changes in the weather always resulted in more joint pain for Franck, and as winter now crept through the front door, he once again felt a numbing of his knees.

"That poor girl. I cannot bear to think of what happened. It makes me so sad. Tell me Franck, who was it that found Tom Madder?" she enquired, as she shook her snowy head slowly from side to side.

"Old Joshua Mouton," Franck replied, "Fancy that! He has only been off Sable twice this past ten years and he finds Tom nearly dead in the bottom of his boat. If he hadn't seen him, Tom would be halfway to Newfoundland by now."

Joshua Mouton complained constantly about being stuck on Sable. He hated being land-bound; he felt he was viewed as an inconvenience, someone barely tolerated by the other islanders. Many sailors held a similar stance, and would rather die at sea than live out their final days on land. When, however, the opportunity had presented itself to sail to Lunenburg for supplies as a favour to Garrett Folcher, Joshua had whined so much that Garrett had nearly told him to forget it.

However, the old man still had his sea legs and was quickly focused on the job in hand. He was well into his seventies and a little frail. It was lucky that he had retained a certain core strength gained from a lifetime of constant toil. He actually stopped moaning to himself as he departed Freetown, and the small supply boat began cutting through the waves with ease. He called out as the boat picked up speed. He had missed the open water and was exhilarated to be back amongst the tides. He felt young again, as he had when he had fished the Grand Banks.

"Garrett Folcher, you are a prince among men for talking

me back to the boats. I thank you for that." Joshua would never actually thank Garrett in person, but it was good to feel so alive. He had forgotten how much he loved the smells and sounds of being a mariner. "I love you, my old lady!" he cried out to his mistress –The Atlantic Ocean.

After the storm, the weather was set fair, although it had just started to snow. Not hard, just the kind of precipitation that falls slowly. The drifts of powder floated down, disappearing into the blackened depths of the water. It was cold; not unusually for late October, yet old Mouton was able to keep warm through the rigours of controlling the vessel on open water.

It was just past an hour into his voyage when Mouton spied Jacob's battered dory floating out towards the open ocean. The sails had gone, as had the rudder, and Mouton thought the boat was empty. It did not yet register that it was the dory that Tom Madder had so expensively purchased for his funny little boy.

"What a salvage I have before me. I could sell this beauty and, after a lick of paint, it will feed me for twelve months or more," the old mariner said out loud. He altered his course, heading directly towards the seemingly abandoned dory.

As he pulled alongside, he could make out a sound he recalled from his years out at sea. A haunting sound, that both saddened his heart and worried the old-timer. The haunting cry of a Great Black-Backed gull – the bird known by sailors as the coffin carrier – filled the air.

Holding the side of the drifting dory with one hand, the

experienced mariner used a trusty round turn and two half hitches to secure the two vessels together. Once secured, Mouton was able to stand up and look directly into Jacob's dory. There, lying still face up on the bottom of the boat, was Tom Madder. There was a large gash in his face that was so deep you could see his jawbone visible through a mass of ragged tendon and muscle.

Mouton was used to seeing terrible sights from his long career as a fisherman on the banks. He had once seen a sailor have his whole arm ripped from his body like a hungry man ripping off a chicken leg. The unfortunate sailor, who, alongside Mouton, was part of the crew of a large steamer, had secured a rope to the wrong line. This line was attached to a chain that was in turn attached to the main anchor; he had unwittingly coiled the rope round his bicep. The ship's Captain gave the order for the anchor to be dispatched to the depths and as it hurtled down so the man's arm followed. The crew stood in horror as the sailor's body writhed on the deck, a fountain of blood spurting from a main artery in rhythm to the man's beating heart. It was cauterised and the sailor survived the trip back to port only to lose his life one month later in a drunken brawl over his liability as a fisherman.

As Mouton stood, balancing between the two craft, the image before him was quite shocking. It was plainly obvious to Joshua that something had been eating Tom Madder's face. Again, the strangled cry of the great seabird. Joshua's gaze was drawn to Madder's arm, where, at the end, in a vice-like hold, a bloody hand gripped the gull itself by its leg. It had pecked at the hand repeatedly. There had been no yielding of the grip however, and Joshua knew that Madder must either still be alive or his hand frozen in a death grip, imprisoning the giant bird.

"My Lord, what in God's name is this?" said Mouton in wonder.

The gull turned its head, as if to look Joshua in the eye. With less grace than perhaps an old sailor should have, he clambered on board the dory. It was hard to find a good footing, given that Madder's large frame had taken up most of the space in the boat. Joshua stumbled. He held out both hands, using the stricken Madder to break his fall. His full weight landed on the king of the fishermen's chest. He was now lying face to face with Tom Madder, closer to the weeping hole than he liked. If he hadn't been profoundly deaf, he would have heard the minor murmur that Tom gave off. The old man quickly pushed himself up so that he was now on all fours, like a wild dog protecting his quarry. Turning over so that he was now sat on Tom's stomach, with his scrawny legs only just fitting into the space between the stricken man and the sidewall of the dory, he let out a great chuff of air. This was tiring for one so old.

The gull trapped by Tom's hand was not only scared but also extremely agitated. It started to flap its wings in a frenzied attempt to break free. Feathers came loose and floated alongside the flurries of snow. The poor bird cried out. A guttural wail asking for help from this mariner, stumbling about within the dory.

"Okay, okay, I'll get to you soon enough." Joshua had forgotten how big a seagull could be, especially one only an arm's length away. He carefully, in rhythm with the boat's movement, got to his feet, and thought about how best to release the bird. As he reached over, the bird pecked ferociously at his outstretched hand.

"Okay, sweet one, I know you think I am here to hurt you. You have to trust this old sailor. Be calm for me, there's a good girl." He had adopted a soothing tone with his croaky voice, yet the angry gull was having none of it. Joshua retreated, searching for something to wrap around his hand to protect it from the gull's constant jabbing. The dory was empty apart from man and bird, so he drove his hand into Tom's jacket pocket, where he found a small ball of fishing line, encased in an oily rag. Tossing the line into the bow of the boat, he tied the rag over his knuckles and once again approached the gull.

It took some effort for the old man to prize open the hand imprisoning the seagull. Once released, rather than fly off, the gull hopped onto the top of the transom. It cocked its head to one side, looking at him.

"Why do you not fly off, my pretty girl?" It was as if some acknowledgement had passed between the bird and the fisherman. What a tale this would make when Joshua arrived back on Sable. He thought people would think him mad and dismiss his tale as exaggerated hogwash. Yet the gull sat there still, eyeing the old man up and down.

"Reckon you and me have a lot in common, bird. Seen the same harshness on these seas, that's what I think, my girl. We'd best be on our way, I have to tow this dory back home. There's not going to be many fishermen around these parts crying over Tom Madder's death, I can tell you that!"

Joshua stood up and started to climb back aboard Garrett Folcher's supply boat, which he had tethered to the dory. As he moved, the gull scuttled along the timber that curved round to the bow of the Madder vessel. Joshua quickly double-checked that he had secured a line to Jacob's dory, and sat at the tiller of his smaller boat.

"Let's be off, my lovely," the old man said to the gull. Strangely, it had not flown off already. He looked at the pile of supplies that should be destined for Lunenburg dock, then back at the dory, stood near to Tom Madder, whom he now presumed deceased. He calculated that he was at the mid-point between Sable and the mainland. With a great pull on the tiller, the boat turned slowly and headed straight for Lunenburg. Tom Madder would surely not care a jot that the supplies were to be delivered first.

It would take Joshua more than two hours to get to port. Due to lighter winds than normal and the added weight of the dory to pull, the pace he set was pedestrian at best. The small sail of his boat billowed like a giant's cheeks full of air, straining with the effort of propelling the two boats toward Lunenburg.

Three fishermen stood at the end of the main dock, looking out to sea. On the horizon, Joshua Mouton, his boats, and a gull cast dark silhouettes against the blackening sky.

"There's another storm brewing," a stocky fisherman said, as he pointed to a grey shadow in the distance, cascading ice and snow from the heavens. "Good job the winds don't blow, or else them boats would be surfing in."

"Must be the Sable express out yonder," a taller man in oils quipped.

Mouton was working the boat, tacking in and out of the currents. He could see that his progress was causing entertainment for the otherwise redundant fishermen on the edge of the wooden dock. "Bloody inbreeds, Miss Gull," he shouted to his feathery companion, who had hunkered down on a cross thwart in the other boat.

Reaching the haven of the bay of Lunenburg enabled Mouton to plot a good course, and his great skill brought both boats parallel to where the men stood. "Aye, you on the dock," he shouted.

"Aye yourself. Two boats at once, Joshua Mouton? You planning on draining your wallet in the supply stores, man?" The stockier fisherman sarcastically replied.

"Nope, I bring me a dead man in my new boat!" He proclaimed with pride. As the boats slowed to a stop, the large gull launched itself away from the rear dory, startling the men. As fishermen, they held these birds in awe, and in unison they all spat onto their boots. Superstition was rife among them.

"Good God, Mouton, what bad luck do you wish to bring

to this port? We don't need another hurricane so soon after Saxby."

"Nonsense, just piss off." Mouton was full of hubris, and had little time for the poor humour of these infantile, idle fishermen.

The old man felt deeply saddened by the gull's sudden departure. Perhaps it had stayed with him until he was safely in port – repayment, in part, for releasing the great seabird from the dead man's grip? At least that was how Joshua would recall it, when asked to tell his tale over a glass of rum or two.

13

Frozen

ELI JAMES HAD SPOTTED THE DARK figure standing alone on East Beach from a fair distance. He had not alerted his father to its presence as they had passed by; rather, he had distracted him by pointing toward something in the opposite direction. He instantly knew who it was from the stark outline against the predominantly grey background of ocean and snow-laden clouds. Cole Haas looked like a pepper pot with his black robes and clerical hat.

Eli needed to talk to the reverend and would return alone, after he and his father had unloaded the supplies they were transporting to the lighthouse.

It was early November, and temperatures on the island had plummeted to ten below. The wind chill made it feel much colder. Winter 1869 was going to be one of the coldest on record, and already the digit-numbing chill held a firm grip on Sable.

Fishermen normally used to the hardships born of winter storms were struggling to cope with such constant low temperatures. Many of them looked down at blackened toes as they removed their thick socks to bathe – a result of frostbite attacking their extremities. Even rubbing them was painful; there was many a grimace behind the doors of the assorted cottages as wives tried to tend to their husbands' feet. During December, the sea froze around the bay altogether, quite literally cutting the island off, as small boats failed to break through the icy crust. Eli found the frozen carcass of a dead harbour seal stuck in the sea ice early one morning. Scavenger birds were unable to crack through the solid blubber, and the seal would remain intact until the thaw came in March.

Ice was already beginning to form at the very edge of the surf, as Cole Haas stood alone on East Beach that November morning. The seashore mainly consisted of small, smooth pebbles, although there were also a few areas of fine sand dotted along the coastline, much like circular islands in the sea of stones. Being so cold, the granular surface was frozen solid, much like sandpaper. Father Cole Haas was standing barefooted on one of these small islands. He was talking to himself, aiming his words to an imaginary being.

Since Robert James had told Cole Haas that his daughter had been violently murdered, the reverend had not spoken to any living being. He had been seen on a daily basis, shuffling about Freetown, carrying on a dialogue with a more ethereal being than man. It had been two weeks since that fateful day, and islanders were worried about the state of Cole's mind.

"Poor man, he's gone mad, plain and simple. It's such a crying shame. God should look after his own in a better way, don't you think?" Mabel Zwicker said at a gathering of the fishermen's wives. As one, the women agreed with the sentiment offered by Mrs Zwicker. In actual fact, everyone on Sable felt sorry for Haas. It was an awkward situation; not many people knew what to say after such a loss. They were actually more familiar with consulting the priest for comfort and advice in times of grief or pain. None had found the courage to address him directly, to console him in his hour of need. How they wished that Tom Madder – even though few felt a kinship to the King of the Fishermen – were on hand to, at the very least, talk to Haas. They left him to his mad mutterings, deciding that perhaps Cole would eventually find solace from a higher being. At least, that is what they hoped.

The last two Sunday services were noted for the complete absence of the father, and members of the congregation – which had swelled for some reason – were left to their own devices. There was no contingency plan regarding spiritual matters, and no message had yet been sent to St. Norbert's in Lunenburg informing them of the ongoing tragedy. The church – also the home of Cole Haas – had remained silent on both Sundays, until one by one, members of the congregation had stood up and left. None of them knew that Cole was upstairs in the far corner of Nancy's now-redundant bedroom, wildly scribbling on pieces of paper.

It was during the first significant fall of snow on the Tuesday morning that Eli spied Cole Haas striding towards the lighthouse on South Shore. He was wearing his simple cassock, black and slightly frayed at the edges. His shoes were well-worn and normally only used when he delivered his sermons from inside Dove House. His pale hands protruded from dark sleeves. He wore no outer coat, no gloves or boots, as he made his way along the bluff.

As they were unloading the cart just outside the lighthouse, Eli was hatching his plan to return to East Beach and speak to Cole.

"Father, I have to go back to Freetown. I left one of my schoolbooks on Miss Robert's desk and need it; I think there is a test tomorrow. Can I use the pony?" he asked sheepishly. He knew his father bemoaned his lack of application when it came to his ongoing education. The promise, therefore, of actually applying himself in readiness for a potential examination was unlikely to be met with any counter-argument.

"How many times have I told you, Eli? You really need to pull your finger out! Miss Roberts has already told me that you and Jacob mess about a lot. Now that Nancy has gone, I don't know how she will cope, instructing you. I want you to have choices in your life. You need an education to get away from Sable." Robert regretted mentioning Nancy. It was inappropriate and he wished he had not said it. He also knew that without her steadying influence, Eli's chances of gaining a sound education were most definitely reduced.

Eli was really shocked by his father's unexpected admission. He had always believed that his destiny was to follow the family tradition and become the lighthouse keeper. He thought this was what his father had always wanted. He had rarely given consideration to a life away from Sable. He most certainly had no instinct out at sea, so had never imagined a life as a fisherman.

"You'd best be quick. I don't want you out all day. Besides, we have to winterise the house before the weather really turns. Be careful, son, I'll expect you back within the hour."

"I promise to come straight back," Eli lied.

Heading straight towards East Beach, Eli pressed the pony hard along the coast track, which had become rutted in recent days. He pulled up the collar of his coat to protect himself from the high winds common on the exposed trail. He knew one mistake could send the cart and him over the edge, to a watery end. The pony – a black and white mare – opened her eyes so wide that she seemed startled. A soft, milky sweat covered her withers, and the harness across her back creaked under the strain of speed. Focused on the croup, Eli hoped that the pony being used to the track would afford him a safe passage down to the beach. The cart was quite primitive in construction; Eli grunted as he bounced up and down on the well-worn seat. If there were any witnesses to his journey they would have wondered why he travelled so fast on such a precarious coastal path. Eli, the horse, and the cart created a strange silhouette against the horizon as they bounced along.

Slowing as he approached the thinner track down to the beach, he looked for the reverend. Standing, legs apart, he gave a short, sharp tug on the reins. The pony stopped, blowing bursts of air from her large nostrils.

"Whoa, girl," Eli yelled, simultaneously making a guttural clicking sound that the pony knew. Steam rose from the small horse, and Eli patted her hindquarters, before loosely tying the rein around a large stone. He scanned the beach again for signs of the crazed Cole Haas. At the far end, just as the beach curved into low scrubby bushes, Haas stood, looking out to sea. Eli noticed the familiar shaking of shoulders; he instantly knew the reverend was delivering words. Not a living soul was present, yet the preacher carried on his tirade with gusto.

Eli approached with caution. The sound of displaced pebbles belied his stealthy manoeuvers. He waited for the holy man to acknowledge his presence – nothing. Cole seemed oblivious to his very existence. Eli was now so close to the poor man that he could hear his every word. Holding his breath, he listened.

"What is it that you expected from me? I gave you everything, for what in return? My faith, for nothing? Hardly a good deal, is it, Lord? Time was when I held you close to my heart, my saviour – tosh! It was surely my right to have a family and for you to keep them safe. Pain and lies, that is what I have. My poor girls did not deserve the path you laid out for them. You could have taken me. That, I would have understood. I cannot forgive you for what you have allowed, when beggars and thieves live a full life. You make me sick. I denounce you for what you are – a deceiver, a fraudster. You, the tormentor of good men and women who try to live by your rules, written in your book. What is the point? Holy Bible – the book is a sham." As he spoke, he tore pages from his own copy of the holy book, given to him when he was a boy. He held them above his head, before allowing the stiff coastal wind to lift the gossamer sheets upwards, swirling.

Eli saw that there were many pages strewn across the beach. He waited for a suitable moment to interrupt.

"Mr Haas? It's Eli, Eli James."

Cole still failed to acknowledge Eli's presence, instead turning full circle and continuing his conversation with the sea. His hands trembled as he waved them about, palms open to receive an imaginary hand from on high. Eli could see that Cole was too cold. His bare feet were turning blue, his hands were splitting, wounds wedged open by the cold winds. Traces of congealed blood enveloped his fingernails. Having not slept at all since the death of his daughter, his hopeless eyes were sunken in a troubled face. He was a sorry sight.

"Mr Haas, it's me, Eli James. Are you alright? I need to talk to you."

"What? Yes, oh, yes, three little children playing on the fields. Does your mummy know you're here? Nancy told me you'd come."

Eli was confused and taken aback by this last statement. The reverend had adopted a childlike voice and was obviously in a distressed state. Eli had not bargained on feeling so sorry for him, and took a few seconds to gather the confidence to re-commence their strange conversation. "Reverend, I have something I need to tell you. And it's about Nancy and Jacob."

Cole looked Eli directly in the eye. "You know, life here is so hard. A man once said to me, if your life is like a jail sentence then you must hastily break out of prison. Hmm, beach walking, are you? Come to look for shells? I myself am having a conflab with your maker! What do you think of that?"

"What on Earth are you talking about? I must tell you something. I have carried it within me for too long. Please listen to what I have to say."

Cole moved closer to Eli, tilting his head in such a way as to encourage whispered words. Eli obliged, speaking quickly. Message delivered, he straightened his back, tugged on his collar to afford him a little extra warmth and left.

Eli departed East Beach more quickly than he had arrived. He headed back along the track he had walked down earlier, reaching the pony within minutes. He was quickly astride, and disappeared on his way, back to the lighthouse.

The parting words whispered to him as young James had walked away from the sandy spur stunned Cole Haas, who still stood, statuesque. He looked like a man stuck in the middle of a bloody battle, speechless and numb. Lost. The words cut through the storm in his head; he now knew who had killed his Nancy.

Cole wanted to feel the pain of pure grief, to dwell in the rawness of pain. It would be his way of keeping close to Nancy. Letting go of his grief would mean letting go of her. And besides, why let go of it? There is no point. The church had taught him all along that forgiveness would enable him to relinquish his pain. Absolve those who sin against you, that's what a righteous man is supposed to do isn't it? Yet no forgiveness would bring him peace.

"There must be nothing beyond this life, we just rot, turn to dust. I will never see my loved ones again. I denounce you, you who have betrayed my beliefs, and I hate you for that." He was exhausted, and fell to his knees. He wanted to sleep. His anger at God had left him hollow. A feeling of emptiness welled within.

"I hate you, Lord." The sound of the incoming tide drowned his sobbing, as his reddened eyes fixated on the horizon. Stupefied, he finally succumbed to the chill in his heart. With painful extremities, and toes and fingers blackening, he would soon be as solid as granite. He tried to mouth words, but none came to the poor man who had lost everything, including his hope.

Within three hours, as the darkness reached night's mid-point, the constant sound of water rushing over pebbles echoed around the bay. Cole Haas managed to whisper a final clutch of words before he froze to death.

"God, forgive me. I was wrong to ever doubt you."

Could anyone be certain that in his dying moment he had re-found his faith? Who knows? Only a soul just before the end could tell us for certain, when perhaps it would be too late to say out loud. Those still living can only guess the answer to this mystery, and such assumptions are more often than not wrong.

As the sun rose on another freezing morning on East Beach, any passer-by would see the Reverend Cole Haas cross-legged and barefoot, frozen in time. The reddish glow of the dawn light illuminated the tragic scene. His black hat stuck atop a waxy white face, held there by fingers of ice. A single tear caught part-way down his right cheek, frozen as a small globule. His eyebrows dusted with ice, small balls of white attached to each delicate strand of hair.

14

Flood

"UNTIE THE ROPE. UNTIE THE BLOODY bloody rope, boy, can't you hear me?" Riggins bellowed, from the mouth of the money pit. After gaining no response whatsoever, he grew irked that his plans were further delayed. Riggins expected things to be done his way, and had little sentiment when they went awry. He started to tug at the rope in sudden bursts. "Was that boy born stupid, Mr Thomsen, or has he suffered too many bangs on the head?"

Thomsen, who was busy untying the rope from around his waist and tethering it to another tree stump, slowly walked over to the pit, and, in a moment of contemplation, scratched the top of his head. He placed his hand around Riggins's arm, causing his irritated companion to let go of the rope.

Deep below, in complete darkness, Jacob sat on the muddy floor. He was afraid. He could sense small movements on the rope, fearing that he may be stranded forever in this dark grave, he stood up and contemplated climbing back to the surface. It was a tough choice, to stay in the pit or potentially suffer at the hands of Riggins. He had never been completely comfortable with the dark, and the scurrying sounds around him only enhanced his fear. Given the effort required to climb up to the surface unassisted, he slumped back to the floor and decided to wait for a short time. They would surely help him although he had forgotten the words Riggins had barked at him before he was lowered into the pit.

"Jacob, when you reach the bottom, untie the rope and we will pull it up to send down some equipment. Do you understand that?" Riggins had said.

Back at the surface, Riggins was losing his mind. "Thomsen, you shall have to pull him out, there's nothing more we can do. I will wring his neck, the little bastard. Does he not realise that we could be discovered at any moment? There is much to do." He tugged on the rope again. "Right, bring him up now!" His mood was becoming increasingly acerbic, thanks to the seemingly inefficient actions of his colleagues.

Thomsen, already exhausted from lowering Jacob into the pit in the first place, did not relish the prospect of further toil. He hesitated. Impatiently, an agitated Riggins took a grip of the thick rope and started to pull. For such a big man, he possessed only modest strength.

Deep below, Jacob heard the rattle of the small, unlit lantern attached to the rope above his head. It seemed to snap him out of his dream-like state, and he quickly stood up, stepping away from the wooden seat attached to the rope. He was wary of the possibility that he was not alone, and, nervously, his eyes darted towards every corner of the pit. Peering up towards the sky, he could not make out any discernible shapes, let alone the comfort of daylight.

"Hey up there, get me out of here, I can't see anything," he shouted upwards.

Riggins immediately stopped pulling at the rope. "Hear that, Thomsen, what did he say?"

It is a fact that such a length of rope, even with no boy attached, still has considerable weight, and Riggins, unaccustomed as he was to such a task, could not sense if Jacob was at the end of it. Beginning to blow exhausted breaths, he looked to Thomsen to take over.

"Do you think he has done as I told him, and got off the rope? I can't tell."

Thomsen grabbed hold of the rope quickly, gauging the weight of it. He instinctively knew that Jacob was not at the end of the line. Quickly, he hauled the rope, coiling it on the ground in front of his feet.

Riggins, who had removed the cable from around his waist, carried the bundle of tools towards where Thomsen steadfastly worked. He was ready to secure the equipment to the wooden seat. As he moved, there was a clattering metallic sound. Thomsen shook his head when he saw the source of the sound was various implements thrust into the thick belt around Riggins' waist.

Being impatient by nature, Riggins rushed, his fingers trying to keep up with the enthusiasm of his mind. He seemed to give no thought whatsoever to the consequences of the equipment hurtling ninety feet to the floor of the pit. And what if Jacob was lying directly below?

"Thomsen, I cannot trust the waif in this task. Lower me down, then follow me. I am sure you can climb down; you're not scared of heights, are you? Besides, there's no reason to stay up here when we can send the boy back up to keep lookout whilst we find the bounty. He likes you, Thomsen, so he'll stick around."

With that, he straddled the bundle of shovels and torches tied on top of the small wooden seat, adjusted himself, then waited for Thomsen to lower him down into the pit. Riggins started to pick his nose, curiously examining the snot before uncouthly thrusting his finger between his lips. He was a bag of nerves, shuffling uneasily as he waited for Thomsen to begin the hard work of lowering him into the pit.

Slowly, he descended, too excited to feel fear, too angry with Jacob to worry about the strength of the rope. Riggins leaned forward and lowered his voice, which reverberated off the walls. "There's nothing you can hide from a man like Abe Riggins, boy. That's why I sent you down first – you'd better not be hiding something you've found, 'cause I will run you through with my dagger. That would be a world of pain to a skinny shit like you."

Looking upwards, Jacob could see a halo of light surrounding the silhouette of a man about forty feet above him. The distance seemed to play games with his vision. Lumps of grit fell as Riggins gathered momentum. Jacob had to shield his face before retreating into the darkness, away from the shaft. He could sense it would not be long before he would have company. In one way he was glad, as he was very nervous about the source of the scratching in one of the tunnels that led away from where he sat.

The unmistakable sound of Riggins' voice filled the space between them.

"Watch out, boy, I have arrived to take over. If there is a job to be done then I am the man for it. I shouldn't have expected you to manage. Never mind, you will be out of here directly, fella. Thomsen can come down then. You listen well though; if you run off up there, I will find you and tear you apart, do you hear?"

"I've nowhere to run to, Mr Riggins."

"Well think on. If we find the treasure, I may give you a token or two."

With that, Jacob squeezed past Riggins to sit back on the wooden seat and pulled at the rope, hoping that this signal would be fully understood by Thomsen – who would then pull him up to the surface. With a shudder, the rope tightened, and Jacob rose up like a bubble rising in a bottle of ale. He reached the surface in minutes, to find Thomsen doubled over, trying to regain his breath.

"Riggins wants you down there." Jacob pointed to the mouth of the pit. "He seems really angry."

Giving Jacob a knowing look, Thomsen strapped himself to the makeshift wooden seat. He knew Jacob would not have the strength to lower him into the pit alone, so he looped a coil of rope twice around a nearby tree. This would ensure that he himself could use leverage and maintain control of his own descent. At the very least, he would not hurtle into the abyss. Slowly at first, he began to lower himself, waiting for the tell-tale sign that the cable was taut. He had entwined the rope between his stubby fingers, and each digit felt the coarseness of the thick cord. He was not going to let go.

Concentrating diligently on the task, he hadn't noticed that his fingers had begun to lose skin due to the friction caused by his slow but constant fall. As a serpent moves through its underground lair, the rope moved silently through his grasp. As Jacob had before him, Thomsen started to smell the pungent air within the pit. The fresh air abundant above ground was absent, and he decided to breathe through his mouth to negate the odour. He did not care for small spaces, especially underground.

The rope juddered just twenty feet from the bottom of the great excavation. Thomsen's right index finger dislocated, and as the line once again became taut, audible clicks were heard, the joint giving way. The luxation was so painful that Thomsen let out a great wail. He looked down at his finger, which was at a 45-degree angle from his knuckles. He had once known of a sailor that ignored a similar injury, not letting anyone touch the joint as it was too painful. He ended up losing his whole hand due to loss of blood flow and a subsequent infection from where the skin had split from a lack of elasticity. Thomsen acted quickly, clasping the digit with his other hand and pulling upward in a single motion. Tears of pain ran down his cheeks as he looked skywards in search of some relief. This was no easy task, suspended as he was.

Below, Riggins was growing more impatient. He could see his friend's shadowy figure swinging from side to side in mid-air. "Thomsen, quit fooling about, man, get down here right now!" He reached for his trusty hipflask and took a deep toot of the calming elixir. As he returned the flask to his pocket, a falling shovel clipped his shoulder, landing in a plume of dust, barely three inches from slicing through his boot.

"Christ, Thomsen, are you a fucking idiot?"

Above, Thomsen was hanging on for dear life. Unable to control his descent – he was losing hold of the cable that held him – he jerked down foot by foot. With skin rasped from his hands, and a painful dislocation, he decided his best option was to fall quickly to the bottom. He was now only about fifteen feet from the floor of the pit. If he were lucky, Riggins would break his fall. He let go.

Riggins was looking upwards as Thomsen, equipment and all, hurtled toward him. Having no time to move, his friend landed squarely on top of his head.

"Jesus Christ, Thomsen, what the fuck are you up to?"

The two men were entangled; both had minor injuries that could be tended to at a later time. Riggins kicked out at Thomsen as he got to his feet. "You imbecile, this is no place for broken bones. Sometimes I wonder why I involve you in these adventures."

It took some time for his eyes to grow accustomed to the poor light. As the extent of the excavations became apparent, Thomsen was astounded by the complexity of the burrows. It was as if a pack of giant beavers had constructed a maze of interconnecting thoroughfares.

"Come on, Thomsen, there is no time to dally. We have treasure to find. As I see it, there are four tunnels to explore. If we each take two, we should be out of here quickly. I have a feeling that if I wanted to hide my bounty, I would do it down here." Riggins, torch in hand, strode off along the main artery, in an easterly direction.

Having left Thomsen by the main shaft, Riggins pressed on despite his confidence being feigned, determined that his exploration would not amount to folly. Rushing forth like a madman, he looked for signs of loot. He considered again; if he had valuables to hide, where would he conceal them? A more devious mind than his had developed the Oak Island money pit, and so no clues presented themselves.

As he approached the end of the tunnel – which was some thirty feet in length – he noticed that the walls, floor, and ceiling were covered with coir matting. Each end had been nailed into stout oak beams using crude tacks. He ran his fingers over the flattened heads.

"Amazing. Who would have thought?"

Finding a suitably soft area in the wall, Riggins jammed his lighted torch into the pliable earth. This enabled him to investigate his surroundings with both hands.

By pressing against the covering, he could clearly feel indentations, perhaps a secret door, he thought. Desperately needing to see behind the covering, he took out his small dagger from his leather sheath, and drove the blade into the coir. This in turn exposed a panel of wood, some three feet square, which was darkened by dampness. He could smell a strong mustiness in the air as a result of his toil in exposing the hidden wood. To one corner of the panel was a smaller piece of wood protruding from a four inch spilt between the wood and the clay earth. He quickly reached for the iron bar he had stashed in his belt. He wedged the flat end of the bar into one of the small gaps he had felt underneath the surface of the matting. Levering his full weight on the opposite end of the crowbar, he pushed down, hoping for some movement. A great splintering noise filled the tunnel, and this encouraged Riggins to remove the bar and drive it into the widening hole now evident through the material. Excitement filled his mind.

Working at a feverish rate, he tore into the wooden panel. Perhaps, if he were a more cautious man, he would have stopped to notice that one of the large supports holding up the roof had tilted, and the great weight of earth suspended above him had shifted, causing the supports to groan. But the possibility of finding valuables beyond the dead end obsessed Riggins to the extent that fear had momentarily deserted his mind. His sweat-soaked skin glistened in the flickering light. He had removed his outer garments, and was now spearing the end of a shovel into the gap he had created in the wall. He also failed to notice a thick coil of twisted rope, seemingly redundant, looped just under the wooden planks at his feet. Following the course of the rope, it disappeared into the soil, returning to entwine the brace between the side support and the beam going from one side of the passageway to the other.

In the darkness, the sound seemed amplified to deafening proportions as the timber supports collapsed in on themselves. Riggins was pinned against the wall as dirt and dust filled the tunnel. Whoever had constructed this tunnel didn't wish any future visitor to go beyond where he now stood. The thick rope had become so taut that it was beginning to unravel. Riggins, now fully aware that something was wrong, pushed away from the wall and limped into the darkness. He just knew he had to get out of this tunnel immediately. He was lucky that he had not been hit by one of the falling beams. He started to move more quickly, using his outstretched arms to feel his way along.

Whilst running away, Riggins could hear the sound of rushing water backfilling the tunnel he had just left. There was now no turning back. Ahead, he would meet a dead end; behind him, water. His hand gripped tightly the burning stick, which gave off a modest, juddering light; he knew that he would soon be in the dark in this god-awful place. He also knew that if he could not find an exit further down, he was doomed. Who would have booby-trapped the pit? And why, if there was no treasure to be found? The thought occurred to him that perhaps there would be treasure, hidden deep within the labyrinth painstakingly carved out of the earth, here beneath Oak Island. Surely, this was not some humorous hoax; the scale of work alone would have taken years, and to what end?

Riggins looked down at his boots, as water silently rushed over them. He slowly reached down, dipping his index finger into the dark liquid. Placing it between his lips, he grimaced.

"Salt!" He spat out the bitter taste. His bravado sank as the reality of his situation became clear. The tunnel was filling with seawater. Within minutes, the water had covered his calf. At a time when panic would have stricken most men, Abe Riggins simply sat down, resigned to his fate.

Doubt leapt into a mind previously filled to the brim with optimism. Riggins knew now that the treasure myth of Oak Island was just that, a myth, and that he would drown in this tunnel, a poor man. He longed for the touch of Myrna Lee as the water level rose above his chest. He started to sing an old sea shanty, Whiskey Johnny, the one that he always sang after too much ale in the Mariner King Inn.

"Whiskey killed me poor old dad,

Whiskey drove me mother mad,

My wife and I do not agree,

She puts whiskey in her tea,

Whiskey O, Johnny O, Whiskey O, Johnny O,"

His voice was filled with regret and sadness as the water level rose above his shoulders. Singing and spitting could be heard above the gushing sound which filled the tunnel. Thomsen, who was making his way to the shaft, and a means of escape, paused, straining to hear a familiar tune. It was too late for Abe Riggins, who was now fully submerged in the murky, brine-filled water.

Thomsen had taken a route in the opposite direction to Riggins. Something told him he needed to get out of the pit. Now! Racing ahead of the water, which was beginning to flow over his own shoes, he abandoned all of his equipment. He had no light, so felt the way ahead with an outstretched hand. Chasing him along the tunnel like a guard dog protecting its quarry, the water was flowing much faster. Not many things could frighten a man like Thomsen, but the darkness and amplified sound of the rising water caused him to panic. Trying to locate a safe way out, he hadn't the time to give thought to poor Abe Riggins, who quite clearly would perish as the space between the two men and the way out was almost fully filled with water.

The rushing water now began to backfill Thomsen's tunnel. His heavy footsteps resonated like the banging on a drum. Picking up speed, he forged his way forward. Though disorientated, he knew that his only hope for survival would be to get back to the main shaft and climb up – away from the water. He could see, just ahead, the dim glow of torchlight from the torches Riggins had placed along the main artery. They were starting to go out. A lack of air had nullified the fires, which were being snuffed out one by one. He scratched his head, forgetting the injury to his hand and wincing at the sharp pain. The nail on his forefinger had been completely ripped off, and the blood looked as if he had dunked his finger into a pot of ink. He now had a decision to make. Keep going, hoping that this route led to the exit, or run back to where he'd come from and hope that there was another way out. He decided to head straight into the flow of water.

To head directly into the source of danger was an unnatural action. Most would just flee the opposite way, running blindly to certain death, stranded in a dead end. Thomsen, however, surmised that his only chance was to run toward the rising water, and find the opening that led back to the rope and survival. Slowing to a walking pace, he had to remain careful that when he placed his feet it was on firm ground. To twist his ankle now would diminish his chances of getting out. Yet finding firm ground was becoming increasingly difficult, now that the water was higher than his knees and rising. Remaining optimistic, he strode on, feeling his way with both hand and foot.

It wasn't long before the water had reached waist level. If he did not locate the rope soon, it was over. For the first time, he considered he may not get out, and reflected on his life. He had expected to drown out at sea, swimming with mermaids like many a mariner before him. To die underground, as Riggins had, filled his heart with sadness. A loud cracking noise shook him, as one of the larger timbers behind him split, and with it an avalanche of mud and debris fell, blocking the path he had just travelled upon.

Despair knocked vociferously around his head, trying to break its way in. Giant, slow strides pushed Thomsen forward. He could feel the weight of the water pushing against his leg muscles.

"This way, it has to be." he said, to no-one. "I will not die down here." At last, a break; his wet hands felt the tunnel open up to his left. Quickly, with his back pressed against the wall, he shimmied towards salvation. Within a few paces, he saw the pale shaft of light from the surface, and there it was, like a line directly from God himself. The rope swayed gently as the water swirled about Thomsen's body.

Jacob peered into the pit one last time, trying to see deep into the chute. So much had happened to him these past few days that he cared not if anyone should emerge from the depths of the great hole. Indeed, he half expected no-one to; death had gripped his tailcoat and was now consuming all who knew him. He would not miss Riggins; he would, however, feel remorse should Thomsen perish in the money pit. Turning away, he was ready to leave Oak Island, to travel on to a new destination. He knew he needed to move on, to figure out what he should do next. Not back to Sable; perhaps to the provincial capital? Perhaps in Halifax he could disappear into the crowds, fade into the background, be insignificant in a sea of people. Shake death from his being. Pass it to some other poor, unsuspecting individual.

Dressed in rags, and cold to the bone, Jacob knew in his heart that the time had come to leave this place. He needed warmth and a change of fortune. He had seen too much death for one so young. His soul was blackened, his body battered. Mother, Nancy, Father, Riggins, and Thomsen, all gone.

15

Discovery

"HELP ME!" CAME A CRY FROM the dark, stopping Jacob firmly in his tracks. Such an unusual-sounding voice, like no other he had ever heard. He turned and walked back towards the sound emanating from the mouth of the pit.

"Jacob," the thin voice cried out again, summoning assistance.

"Who's there?" Jacob called back. He, quite naturally, did not recognise Thomsen's voice; he thought it belonged to a small child. "Hello, who's there?" he shouted again, his voice echoing abundantly in the pit.

"Jacob, please help me, I cannot hold on for much longer."

Scanning the area immediately around the mouth of the great hole, he noticed one loop of thick rope remained, stacked against the pile of equipment not taken into the pit by Riggins. Quickly, he dragged it over to a tree nearby, and tied one end around the trunk. Taking hold of the loose end, he brought it to the side of the money pit, tossing it over the edge.

Thomsen was spitting dirt from his mouth, as his bodyweight loosened the earth from around the tree root he held in his bloody hands. One false move would result in him falling to his death. The rope thrown by Jacob hit Thomsen squarely in his face.

"Christ, boy, help me, not hinder me!"

Given that Jacob was so small, there was simply no way that he could pull Thomsen up and out into the daylight. Thomsen was at least twice his weight, and even if there were something sturdy to lever the rope through, the task would be futile. Gasping for air to fill his aching lungs, Thomsen knew this, and despite his exhaustion realised that he had to climb up the slippery walls himself. The rope would help, but the cuts on his hands made it hard for him to gain a firm grip.

"You can make it, Thomsen. I know you can, just take your time," Jacob yelled encouragingly. He wished he possessed the strength to save this man at the end of the rope. It was important to him to help save at least this one person, perhaps repaying his part in the deaths of the aforementioned. "I will not let you fail!"

As he looked back into the pit, Thomsen could just make out the dark, swirling water. It was as if the floor was alive, moving as one with the tide. He thought of Riggins' body, which would be bloated and battered, sucked into some unfathomable crevice, never to be seen again. His bloodied fingers sought soft, permeable holds in the walls of the chute. The other hand held the rope. He was so tired, tired enough to not be able to lift his own bodyweight. Herculean effort was required. The need for a foothold to aid him in pulling his own body the forty feet to the surface was dire. His feet flexed, pushing sideways to gain traction. Slowly, he pulled, face covered in sweat and tears, his straining muscles bulging as he rose one foot at a time. It took him nearly one hour to get to the top. There, Jacob – who had constantly encouraged him – opened his arms to greet him as if he was seeing the last man on earth.

"Thomsen, I knew you could do it." Jacob was ecstatic, finally, a life saved rather than doomed.

For poor Thomsen's part, the exertions had taken their toll on him. He lay face down in the mud, never wanting to see any treasure pit again. Thomsen was familiar with hard work, but the toil he had endured on this longest of days had left him exhausted. Before he could contemplate moving, a period of repose was a must. As he lay in the mud, his legs quivered in spasm, as lactic acid coursed through his system.

Jacob, meanwhile, was relieved. He didn't want to be alone; he didn't feel like talking, but he wanted company, he supposed – in fact, he didn't know what he wanted. He just knew that he needed help, and Thomsen – talking or not – was the sort of friend that could help him.

As the sun disappeared behind the red spruce trees, they left the beach together. Walking down the dirt track that cut through the trees along the causeway that joined Oak Island to the Western Shore, they cautiously approached the main thoroughfare. Not wishing to warrant any attention, they moved on in silence, only occasionally looking at each other for endorsement. They need not have worried; during winter, the woods were deserted. Although undecided on which way they should go, they both arrived at the same conclusion; they needed to find shelter before the temperature dropped further. To the left, Mahone Bay, to the right, Chester, Halifax, and passage overseas.

"Best to make camp before it gets cold. You gather some wood for a fire and I will make a shelter over there, just beyond the first line of trees." Thomsen pointed with his splintered finger, towards a place where some of the trees had overhanging limbs away from the path. "If anyone comes, we will be able to see them before they see us."

Jacob returned after a short time, with a pile of dry sticks he had gathered, throwing them on the floor in front of the makeshift camp. Thomsen was a very resourceful man, having gained a lot of knowledge about survival during the years he had spent as a for-hire deckhand. Using two of the smaller sticks, he whittled the end of one into a sharp point and, with the other, carved a notch at the midpoint. He then placed some of the fine wood shavings next to the notch and began to rub the pointy stick between his palms. Jacob looked on, fascinated by the activity. Within minutes, a fire had sparked into life. At least they would have warmth tonight.

As they sat in front of the burning fire, Thomsen handed Jacob a dry biscuit and a chunk of dried meat, the origin of which Jacob dare not guess. Jacob started to chew, slowly, even though he was famished and would have gladly eaten almost anything. The meat had a strange, tangy taste that was barely palatable. Thomsen then set a bashed tin can filled with water just above the fire. He desperately wanted coffee to revive his senses. The grounds were old but he cared little, as long as it was hot and full of caffeine.

"So, what is your story, young Jacob Madder?"

"I would tell you, Thomsen, but I fear you will despise me if you know the truth."

"I have seen a lot of bad things in my life, hung around with bad men, evil men, who would cut your throat as quick as say good evening. I am sure your tale will not make me lose sleep."

"Why do you choose not to talk? I believed you a mute, and it is strange to hear your voice," Jacob said, trying to change the subject.

"Oh, this and that. I have my reasons, but as I asked first you must tell me your tale."

"I think I killed Nancy. I am ashamed to tell you. My father was taking me to the constable when the storm hit us and I was thrown overboard. I didn't help my pa, and now he is drowned and I am wrongly allowed by God to still breathe when it should have been me that perished."

"You say you think you killed Nancy? And who was she?"

"My friend, my beautiful friend."

The fire spat an ember, and something moved in the woods behind them, causing them to stop talking and turn their heads.

"Raccoon, or maybe deer, nothing to bother about," said

Thomsen, as he tended the receding flames of the fire by adding more of the dry sticks. "Go on."

"Eli and I had drunk some hooch – I have never had any before, I swear – then Nancy came over and...I just can't remember, it was terrible." Tears welled in the young boy's eyes as he spoke.

"Try hard to remember what happened next Jacob, it could be the key to getting to the truth."

"It was horrible, the drink, I mean. My head ached and I couldn't see anything clearly. The room was spinning. I remember Nancy being annoyed with me, she called me stupid or something and she went to the toilet." Jacob was trying to focus, his furrowed forehead and pursed lips making him look ten years older. "I can't remember, it's too horrid."

"Close your eyes and take yourself back to that moment, Jacob. Drink only dulls your senses; the truth will be hiding in some uncharted corner of your mind."

"I woke up and there was silence. The house was dark and very cold. My back was sore. I was lying on the floor at the bottom of the stairs. I didn't know where Nancy or Eli were."

"Who is Eli?"

"Eli is my school friend. He was the one who suggested we take my dad's drink."

"So you couldn't find this Eli, then?"

"No, there was no-one about. I shouted out to see if they would come, but nothing. My head was hurting, Thomsen, the ache was unbearable."

"Dehydration." Thomsen was now leaning in so close that Jacob could feel the exhaling of his breath. "What happened next?"

"I found a lantern, looked in all the rooms downstairs, and found them to be empty. I then went upstairs." At this point Jacob stood up, as he retraced his movements on that night. "I saw nothing until I noticed the door to my bedroom was closed. I always leave it open, never closed. When I opened it, that's when I saw her on the floor. The most terrible sight I ever saw. Her face was contorted." He fell down in front of Thomsen, clutching his face as he recalled poor Nancy's lifeless body. Sobbing, he continued. "Her mouth was full of fishing line, her eyes so dark, yet looking beyond me. There was blood and mess, and the smell was metallic and strange. I couldn't stand it, so I ran past the lighthouse and hid up near the Field Of Souls."

"Jacob, did you notice any unusual marks on your hands? Cuts or bruises maybe? Perhaps your shoulders ached more noticeably?"

"I don't remember, Thomsen. I just ran as fast as I could. I hid behind the wooden bows and it was so cold. My legs and back were a bit sore, but not my shoulders." Jacob looked at his hands, which were in a bit of a state after the storm and the money pit. It was hard to recall if they were damaged before, yet… "I remember some blood on my hands, Thomsen, but it wasn't mine, it was Nancy's. I had touched her face before I left. I know I shouldn't have, but she looked so bad, I don't know why I caressed her. Oh, Thomsen, what did I do to her?"

"Jacob, I have one question for you. How tall was Nancy?"

"She was about this much taller than me." Jacob held out the palm of his left hand, six inches above his head.

"And was she a small or large girl?"

"Just about perfect, I thought, what you might call medium build. She had beautiful hair and was so lovely." Jacob paused to think about how much he would miss Nancy Haas; her loss would most certainty create a void in his life.

"Let me see then. Nancy was heavier, taller and stronger than you. Is that correct, Jacob?"

"I guess."

"Think hard, lad, was anyone else with you that evening? Did you see anything out of the ordinary, maybe something not quite right in the house, something changed?"

"I saw Pa's coat on the floor by my feet instead of on the hook where he always put it. The lantern hung by the back door was missing, but nothing else. My head hurts, Thomsen."

"I know lad, but this is important. You recalling what happened will be a great strain. Sit a while and just think, Jacob. The silence will help you, and I should know, I was silent for years!"

As Jacob looked into the dark woods, a strange malaise overwhelmed him. Taking deep breaths, he looked at Thomsen, this unusual companion on whom he now relied.

"One thing that was a little odd, now I think about it. Nancy always wore a sand dollar broach, yet when I saw her on the floor of my room her shawl was loose around her shoulders, not tied at the front with the broach. Her mother gave the broach to her, and to her, it was more precious than gold. I can't believe I even noticed it wasn't there. It probably means nothing."

"Everything means something, Jacob. See, the thing I cannot understand is that you say Nancy was upstairs in the house, and presuming that you would have heard something if she was killed there, she must have been carried upstairs after the fact, past you. From what you say, she would have been hurt badly. She would have screamed, cried out for help, which would have brought attention that no killer would want. I do not believe that you could have carried her upstairs, Jacob, you are too weak and too small. The killer must have at the very least been bigger than Nancy, don't you think?"

Jacob paused, needing to consider this most obvious revelation. "You know what this could mean, Thomsen, don't you? I may not have killed Nancy after all." Jacob was trying to hide his excitement, but soon realised something that turned his mood sour. "If not me, who was it then who killed Nancy?" The thrill of thinking he was innocent had gone as quickly as it had arrived. "I know where I must go now. I must prove that I am innocent, if that's what I am."

"I will travel alongside you, Jacob. You saved me from down there," Thomsen pointed back in the direction of the money pit as he spoke softly. "I promise you, I will stay with you as long as you need me to."

"Thank you, Thomsen. I don't think I could stand this alone." Jacob felt that Thomsen was how he imagined an older brother would be. He had forgotten his desire to understand why his new friend had formerly chosen not to speak. Exhausted, he fell into a deep sleep, his first for several days.

16

Awake

"MOUTON, THIS IS A VERY LONG list, old timer. Are you sure Folcher wants all this at once?" Barnett said, holding the tattered list of goods in his outstretched hand.

John Barnett was the sulky manager of Acadian Marine supplies on Burma Road, to the west of the main dock. He was known locally for his dour sense of humour and bad breath. Many a customer would place an order whilst turning away from the shopkeeper's halitosis. He sported a long, grey beard that often contained various remnants of that day's meals. Even so, Barnett was an institution in Lunenburg, and was well-liked by most.

"Just get the bloody stuff ready and quit your moaning. You'll be paid, no fear about that." Mouton was keen to get back to Sable. His thoughts focused on returning as quickly as he could, with both boats and chattels intact.

"Ok, old man, one of my lads will get this ready for you. I guess you'll want to pop into The Mariner King Inn for a quick libation while you wait?" The store master said, with a voice heavily laden with sarcasm. Everyone knew Joshua Mouton was partial to a nip or ten. "We'll come and get you when your boat needs loading."

"Aye." Mouton ambled out and headed straight for the Historic Inn, where he would relieve them of some rum. Just to keep out the cold, you understand.

Back at the main dock, a young boy wandered about, oblivious to the cold wind now blowing in from the south. His father was busy negotiating with one of the older fishermen over a box of iced winter skate. He had promised his wife to bring home the fish as she enjoyed skate wings cooked in brown butter, as a rare treat. The boy – as youngsters tend to do when a little bored – was poking everything in his path with a twisted birch stick he had found earlier. He looked down at the two dories – side by side – moored to the left edge of the wooden dock, curious about the rough shape beneath a dark grey tarp. He made up his mind there and then to poke at it. Carefully climbing down the wooden frame of the dock, surprisingly mindful of the slippery cross beams, he reached sea level and the two boats. With the stick protruding in front like a lion tamer keeping a distance between a fleshy arm and hard teeth, he slowly moved forward.

Mouton was fast asleep, perched on a corner table at The Mariner King. In front of him was a small glass, alongside a half-empty bottle of Anguilla cask 32. Upon his sleeping face, a smile, displaying his wretched teeth. In his mind, the words he had sung over and over before his alcohol-induced slumber.

"I pity them greatly, but I must be mum, for how could

we do without sugar and rum!?"

"Mouton, wake up fella. You'd better see what a lad has found in your dory," said one of the dockside fishermen – who had witnessed his arrival earlier in the day – as he shook the sleeping mariner. "Mouton, wake up!"

"You bugger, what is the reason you wake me from my rest? I have a hard sail ahead, and you dare disturb me." Mouton was slightly disorientated and very grumpy.

"That dory you brought in."

"Yes? What of it?"

"The fella on the floor of it has woken up."

"You're shitting me. He wasn't breathing, dead as dead he was when I left him, I tell you. So you tell me that Tom Madder is alive? Good God, there goes my new boat." He could not hide his disappointment.

"They have called the doctor. You'd better get down to the dock right away."

"Bloody hell, this day just gets better with each passing minute." Mouton got up, picked up the bottle of Anguilla, and placed it deep in the pocket of his oilskin. He decided that he may just need a little nip later on.

As Joshua arrived at the main dock, he could see the circle of people where he had left the dories. "Crap, just what I need, a bloody circus. There will be too many captains sticking their noses in my business."

The body was heavier than first thought, and three men struggled manfully to lift him from the dory, and place him gently on the dock.

"Give him room!" one of the fishermen cried.

"Fetch Doctor Roberts, this man is barely breathing," said another.

"Where's Jacob?" Tom said, his voice so weak he could barely be heard.

"Who's Jacob?" Dr Roberts enquired of the assembled group. Tom had once again fallen into unconsciousness. "Take him to the inn."

Even at dusk, in the dim candlelight, the marks on Tom's body looked like fresh wounds. Jagged tears cut into his skin and unusual puncture marks dotted both of his hands. The doctor surveyed his patient, looking over spectacles perched on the end of his long nose. Dr Roberts was very familiar with the sorts of injuries suffered at sea, so quickly tended to the seeping sores in a proficient manner.

"Fetch some water; this man is clearly dehydrated and, by the look of it, lucky to be alive."

It was a further week before Tom Madder finally returned to Sable Island. Even the weather was against his departure, and, having made three unfruitful attempts to gain passage, he finally managed to persuade Ben Cross to take him. Cross was an accomplished mariner, completely at home on a rough sea. The rougher the better was his motto. He enjoyed nothing more than to be out on the water when others dared not. In fact, if he happened upon some unfortunate part-time sailor, he would yell and scream at them in an old Arcadian dialect so much so that the frightened seamen would most likely head back to the safety of dry land. Such was Cross's reputation that Tom knew that despite any inclement weather, or worse yet, an ice storm, he would be delivered relatively intact to Sable Island.

Ben Cross waved enthusiastically as he departed Freetown's harbour. He had left Tom alone on the dock. As quickly as they had arrived, he had effortlessly turned the boat through the eye of the wind and sailed away at great speed. Tom stood for a while, watching the boat disappear into the distance. Once the boat was completely out of view, he was struck by the darkening skies that magnificently merged at the far point of the horizon, becoming one with the dark Atlantic waters.

Upon Tom Madder's homecoming there was no parade, no welcome party as he silently, slowly walked to his house from the harbour. The island was still, after all, in shock after Nancy's death, and the islanders were still suspicious of Jacob Madder's disappearance, so much so that whispers flew amongst them.

"His father let him go, that's what I heard."

"Jacob must be the murderer, why else would he disappear?"

As Tom arrived back on the island, Eli James was preparing to leave. He knew he only had a small window of opportunity to beat the ice and have safe passage. If he was lucky, he could make his way up the coast and meet the stagecoach to Halifax. But if the weather really turned, he could lose his life out on the open ocean. He only had meagre supplies; in fact, all he had was about his person, including his father's pocket compass and the money he had "borrowed" from his mother's savings tin. Eighty dollars was carefully wrapped up in parchment paper in his right sock. She would kill him when she found the cash was missing. It had taken her five years to save it up from the modest allowance given to her by Robert. Eli would pay her back at a later date; although he hoped his mother would, in time, let him off.

Eli's plan was simple enough, although in winter any trip would be fraught with danger. He knew Jacob may have perished, and in all probability, this was the case. He had seen the state of Tom Madder when Joshua Mouton had returned from Lunenburg. Water temperatures were brutal at the best of times, so it would be a miracle if his friend had survived. Yet if there was even a slim chance that Jacob was alive, he needed to find him, before anyone else did.

Eli was no expert, and had turned to Mouton to assess what may happen if a body were to be thrown overboard.

"To what end you asking such a question, young fella? If he drowned, he'll be long gone now, eaten by the fish."

"He's my best friend, and deserves me at least trying to look for him."

"Bad weather coming, it's not a good idea to be trawling up and down the coast looking for something you may never find."

"Please sir, help me try. I will only make one sweep up the coast and then get to the mainland for shelter."

"Your pa ok with this?"

Eli knew that his father would ask all the fishermen on the island about his whereabouts, but such was his concern that he steeled himself to take the risk of a beating.

"Sure, he understands why I have to try. I promised him I'd be on dry land by nightfall." Eli tried to give off an air of confidence as he spoke. He would be sailing no matter if Mouton helped or not.

After a moment of deep consideration, Joshua Mouton began.

"Let me see. I found the dory three miles from Lunenburg, and calculating the three tides since, there is a good chance that Jacob would be washed up either on Blue Rocks or Tancook Island, between Mahone Bay and Chester. Like I say though, you've more chance of finding me a new wife than finding him. There it is though. If I were you I would start at Blue Rocks and work east. If you haven't found him by Tancook, get to Chester and stay there until the weather sets fair."

"Right, which way is it to Blue Rocks?" Eli said, as he walked off to get his small skiff ready.

Mouton shook his grizzled head. "He'll be dead by tonight," he muttered under his breath. "Bloody fool!" He needed a drink. It had been a challenging day, and even though he was exhilarated from his labours, he was tired and in need of the comfort of grog. For some unknown reason, he didn't care for Eli James. He thought the boy was both childish and devious. He was still muttering about such things as he took his first soothing tug on the rum bottle.

Eli was not a good sailor. He had been lazy in his youth, dismissing the opportunity to learn the ways of the fishermen from the competent. He did, though, hold enough confidence in his basic seamanship to set off alone early that Thursday morning. The wind was blowing from a westerly direction at 19 knots. Trees along the shoreline were swaying gently, and the moderate waves were tipped with small whitecaps. It was a twelve nautical mile journey to Blue Rocks, and, given his limited speed, it would take him most of the day to get there. Within ten minutes, he had left the shelter of the bay and paused to look back at East Beach. He thought of his final meeting with Cole Haas, shuddered, and returned to the task in hand. The hoisted sail reverberated in the wind, and as quickly as it was raised, the skiff took off at an exhilarating rate.

As they cut a path on top of the waves, sea spray flew into Eli's face. He wiped his brow with the sleeve of the oilskin sou'wester he had borrowed from his father's closet. He dared not consider how angry his father would be as a result of his disappearance. Better to concentrate on finding Jacob, dead or alive. He had no choice in this matter.

After more than three hours sailing, Eli was tired, hungry, and angry that he had not found Jacob. In truth, he had not seen a single other boat during his voyage. His only company had been the occasional inquisitive harbour seal popping up to look at him. Standing up, he could see nothing, only open water. It was then that the futility of his task hit him.

"Shit! What in mother's name am I doing here?" he shouted out loud.

A nearby seal, which was following the skiff, sank swiftly in a swirl of water, startled by this sudden outburst.

Ominously, the sky had darkened and the wind was just beginning to pick up, a sure sign that a storm was heading his way. Eli dipped his hand into the freezing water. "Jesus, I wouldn't want to fall in." The words of Mouton rang in his head, 'Get to Chester before the weather turns'. Thing was, he didn't know where Chester lay, he only knew the way to points further down the coast.

Knowing that he had to move on, he searched for the Gurley pocket compass in the inside of his jacket. It was a lovely thing, cased in its custom-made hardwood box, designed more for surveying than for use out at sea. His father would kill him if he lost it overboard. Carefully, he held it up as he balanced himself, riding the swell by manoeuvring his weight from one leg to the other. He found west, and firmly pulled on the jib, simultaneously turning the tiller to point the boat toward a westerly heading.

Within the hour he finally sighted land. A sight to warm the heart of any sailor, let alone one so inexperienced. He presumed correctly that before him lay the rugged coastline just south of Lunenburg. If Jacob were alive, he would surely have washed up on this part of the coast. It started to snow, the gentle sort of snow that drifts down and lands on your nose.

"Hello there," Eli shouted loudly to a lobsterman winterising his pots on the shore. "Hey, you, on the beach!"

The man looked up from his work. "Who the hell is this clown?" he muttered to himself. "Aye, what ails you?"

"Have you seen a boy, sir? Or maybe heard a tale of one washed up in these parts?"

"This is Blue Rocks, son, no-one washes up on this shoreline. Mind you, I once saw an Oriental fellow, years back it would have been, bloated like a dead whale, he was. Full of gas until he was popped! Jeez, we laughed all week about that."

"Do you think if a boy was thrown overboard out there, he could survive?" Eli pointed out to open water, on the far side of his small boat.

"Blowfish, we called him. Must have been coming here looking for railway work, yet no railways were built 'til last year!" The lobsterman was chuckling away. "What? In these waters, at this time of year, he'd last about five minutes. Why do you ask such a stupid question?"

"I am searching for my friend, Jacob Madder, who fell overboard from a dory nine days ago. His pa made it to Lunenburg, after being rescued by Joshua Mouton, but there was no sign of Jacob. He killed Nancy and is now on the run."

"Slow down, boy. Throwing names at me as if I will know these people, are you a simpleton?"

"Sorry, friend," Eli was unaware he had been rambling.

He was not really apologetic, just wanting information, and if saying sorry helped, so be it.

"You said Mouton, didn't you? I did know a Mouton, fished with him on the Grand Banks, but that was years ago. Two fingers we called him, lost them in a fight over a large woman. Not seen him for years. Thought he'd be living with the fish by now."

"That's Joshua. Joshua Mouton, he lives on Sable now. Will anybody around these waters have seen Jacob?"

"Listen, son, I cannot be expected to know what people round here have seen! I'm too busy for such nonsense, so much to do before the snow covers everything. I suggest you try in Lunenburg. So be on your way and leave me in peace. Oh, and say hello to two fingers when you see him. Tell him Harris says 'fuck you'!" As he spoke, he raised two fingers, in an action Eli had seen many times before.

Eli felt crushed. It had been inevitable that his expectations would be squashed. In reality, to find Jacob anywhere along the seaboard was akin to finding a needle in a haystack. In all probability, he had perished along with countless other men, women, and children thrown into the Atlantic over the years. Eli turned east, and headed the short distance up the coast to Lunenburg.

The moon was deep in the sky as the skiff arrived in the harbour. The snow had become heavier, and Eli stared skyward at the star-like drifts. Being winter, it was not too busy here; only one other boat making its way out to sea, which was just as well, given Eli's failings as a sailor.

He would not have been confident if the bay was full of fishermen going this way and that. He was cold and hungry, yet lucky to have arrived before the predicted bad weather fully set in.

Disembarking, he headed directly to a small wooden hut at the end of Montague Street. The modest shack was used for shelter by those who made their living from trades associated with the sea. Inside, there were five men. Two fishermen, who were sufficiently experienced to know that it would be foolhardy to be out to sea during the storm season. One lobsterman, who, bored of repairing pots, had retreated to the company of others for banter. Of the other three men, one was the harbourmaster and two were traders. The air was thick with tobacco smoke as Eli was blown in; the walls were the colour of faded paper and the single stove offered dry warmth. On top of the firebox stood a dented copper kettle, a single strand of steam snaking its way through the oppressive air, which was thick with pungent smells.

"Jesus, boys, stop with the farting. It's too cold to keep the door open." Brandon Boggs cast an accusatory look at the others. "Who the bloody hell are you?" he continued, this time aiming his question directly at Eli.

"I am Eli James, son of Robert James, the lighthouse keeper on Sable Island. I am looking for my friend, Jacob Madder, who fell out of his dory just off the coast between here and the island."

"Hahahaha!" Every single one of the men within the

hut – which reverberated with the sound of uncontrollable laughter – could not contain their amusement at Eli's statement. Boggs, in particular, was coughing so much that his face had turned crimson; he spat a large ball of sputum, which landed on top of Eli's boots.

"You are too funny, Elbert!"

Eli was too put out to correct Boggs. Shutting the door behind him, he moved deeper into the crowded hut.

"No lighthouse in here, Elton, we won't be in need of a lighter in Lunenburg." Boggs was purposely trying to get a rise from Eli. The others chuckled; Boggs was in his element now that he had an audience.

Eli was getting angry. He had travelled all day, and to find himself the butt of some fisherman's jokes was an experience which was quickly wearing thin. "Look, I just want to know; have you seen anybody washed up along the coastline?"

The lobsterman who was pouring hot water onto a tot of whiskey put the kettle down with a loud twang. "No, son, there has been no-one washed ashore this past month. If I were you, I would travel up to Mahone Bay and the three churches. If anyone knows anything about what you're asking, it will be there."

"How would I get to Mahone Bay today?"

"The stage only runs once a day, every morning at seven. I wouldn't sail up the coast if I were you. A storm is coming, and there are some dangerous rocks just outside the bay. It would take either a fool or a very skilled sailor to attempt that this evening. I presume you are neither?"

"I'd wager the boy's a fool. One dollar to any man who disagrees." Brandon Boggs smiled as he spoke. "Best get the stage coach tomorrow, unless you feel like swimming!"

"Oh, thank you so much, gentlemen, I do wish you a fruitful winter. You have been so much help." Eli could not hide his sarcasm, and left in a hurry. Fishermen were well known for their short tempers, and would not think twice about handing out a beating, especially to a cocky so-and-so like Eli James.

Eli walked back to the skiff to collect his belongings. He would stay at The Mariner Inn for the night and then catch the stage direct to Mahone Bay in the morning.

The clerk on the front desk doubled as the barman. Mr Zwicker owned, managed, and represented one quarter of the staff that ran the Mariner King Inn. The other workers at the inn were the grumpy yet proficient French cook Henri who had arrived in Lunenburg penniless and homeless two years ago, the equally sober handyman, who went by no name at all and was simply referred to as 'handy', and finally Mrs Zwicker, who maintained the guest rooms.

John Zwicker – a sea merchant by trade – had purchased the inn from Dr Bolman during a short visit to Lunenburg. The doctor had constructed the inn in honour of King William, marking his coronation. Zwicker had solely intended to use the property as his family home, and had completed several major renovations with this in mind. Unfortunately, when his brigantine sank with a lapsed insurance policy, he was left with no other choice than to convert his home into a potential money-making business. The inn had become popular as a watering hole, and so in recent years the beautiful Georgian architecture was beginning to show signs of age. However, Zwicker's wife had managed to maintain the guest rooms to a surprisingly high standard. So when Eli was led to his room, he was pleasantly surprised by the contrast to the downstairs, and looked forward to a restful evening.

Venturing into the crowded, noisy bar, Eli, for some reason, grew a little self-conscious. Most unlike him; perhaps it was due to him being exhausted from the journey and the copious effort he had put into not drowning. He purposefully found a seat in a quiet corner of the room. As he sat under candlelight, he began to observe the other people who frequented the inn. It wasn't long before his eyes fixed on a familiar face.

Through the smoke filled room, he saw her. The brief smile that had played on Eli's lips was replaced with a look of disbelief. With a flourish of her shawl, she was gone, out onto King Street. Eli shot up and raced through the crowd, towards the door. It couldn't be her; that was impossible. Before he reached the exit, he knocked the arm of a rough-looking sailor, causing the man to spill his jug of ale. The foamy liquid splashed against the sailor's tatty, black boots.

"Hey, you bastard, look what you've done! Them's me only pair of boots," he said, as he grabbed Eli by the collar. Quick as a flash, Eli took out one silver coin and flipped it, causing the man to let go of him and try to catch the revolving coin. His heart was racing as he burst out of the inn, looking first eastwards down King Street, then turning westward, to see that the street was empty. Frantically, he ran all the way to the corner of Cumberland Street; still no sign of the woman. From just behind him, the sound of bottles rolling across the sidewalk attracted his attention. He turned quickly, to see an old drunk stumbling along, looking for a quiet place in which to rest.

"What you looking at?"

"Oh shut up, you piss head."

Eli ran back towards the Mariner Inn, still finding no sign of anyone. Hunched down, with his hands laid flat against his thighs, his eye was drawn to something shiny protruding out of the mud in the gutter. He reached down to pick it up, studying it closely. It was a circular pewter broach; he turned it in his fingers and noticed the familiar four hexagonal lines of a sand dollar.

Taking one last look along the whole length of King Street, his heart still pounding riotously within his chest, he inhaled a deep breath of the cold Lunenburg air. He must have been mistaken; perhaps it was just his imagination? It could not have been Nancy that he saw in the Mariner King Inn tonight. She was dead. Wasn't she?

17

To Halifax and Beyond

"TAKE ONE STEP FURTHER AND IT will be your last. I won't be hesitating if I have to shoot," came a voice from out of the dark. Thomsen and Jacob froze, as if the voice had supernatural properties that could render any man still.

Thomsen instinctively dropped the small bundle he was carrying and held both arms aloft. Jacob looked at him quizzically, and then followed suit, his bundle making a sharp metallic sound as it hit the ground. They could not see anyone. In fact, they could not see further than ten feet in any direction due to the dense vegetation, so it was hard to gauge where the dark stranger stood.

From just beyond a stack of slowly-rotting timbers, close to where they had made their makeshift camp, there was movement, a rustle. Then, bounding forwards, a large Newfoundland dog approached, at deceptive speed. The dog, black in colour, must have weighed at least seventy kilos, all teeth and fur.

"Skipper, wait!" came a shrill command from out of the dark. "Heel!" The dog instantly stopped in a flurry of dust, and crouched down, as if ready to pounce at any moment. The dog never took its eyes off Jacob and Thomsen, who, more scared than ever, shuffled uneasily, hands still raised toward the sky.

"Stay still, Jacob, I know a little about these dogs. They are gentle giants but can be easily startled, so be nice and quiet, my friend."

"Don't worry, I believe I cannot move at all even if I wanted to!" Jacob whispered in reply.

"What's your business messing up my woods? You one of them treasure hunters, or just here to rob me?" asked the man in the dark. Slowly, a figure presented itself in front of them. It was a man of small build, wearing a large fur hat and coat quite clearly too big for his meagre frame. His face was covered by the shadow of the fur brim, although Jacob did catch a glimpse of a beardless, pointy chin protruding. The voice strangely reminded Jacob of his mother, being more feminine in timbre than a woodsman's. Yet still, he was scared. There was too much to worry about, and Jacob worried about everything.

"We mean no disturbance to you, sir," he called.

"The boy's right, we are just passing through," Thomsen spoke without looking at the figure before them, continuing to focus on the dog.

"Crap! I've seen plenty of folk before ye who said the same thing, then left indeed, but not before taking things that are rightly mine. Thieves, not to be trusted, and you cannot trust anyone these days."

Thomsen looked up as he realised that it was not a man who stood in front of them holding a shotgun, but a young woman.

Evangeline Yung was barely nineteen; to this point she had lived a frequently solitary life, having been abandoned by her parents four years previously. It was not that she was a difficult teenager – only the usual domestic rows occurred – more that her parents gave up, grew weary of the toughness of living in the Maritimes. Work had been scarce for her father, who, being a simple man, found it hard to gain suitable labouring work. His quiet demeanour was often mistaken for arrogance, and locals never felt compelled to help him or his family when hard times hit. He had never served time out at sea, so spent most of his days foraging in the woods, trying to scratch out a living to support his small family. In simple terms, he was lazy, and as such all work seemed a toil and pointless. Her mother was a beauty. She was, for some unknown reason, besotted with a husband many considered a waste of time. To the despair of her family she would have walked through burning fire for him. No-one could fathom why he had such a hold on her; so much so that she was complicit in the abandonment of her only child.

Eve, unlike her indolent father, demonstrated a greater aptitude for working. It took little adjustment for her to eke out a living from her surroundings. She was not only an intelligent girl, but also resourceful. She sold cords of firewood locally, carved odd pieces of timber into saleable children toys, and generally kept busy whilst earning a few cents here and there to get by. She saved every one of the silver coins, keeping them in an old shoe polish tin under her bed. These meagre earnings had enabled her to remain somewhat self-sufficient, living in the small house she occupied in the woods adjacent to Oak Island. Secretly though, she hoped that one day her savings would allow her to travel. For now, she was contented, and approached each day with an enthusiasm that was infectious.

It had been a particularly cold day in the winter of 1865 when she arrived home to find the house empty. No parents, no possessions, other than a small collection of pots and pans sat atop a cast iron stove in the corner of the two-bedroom cabin. Fortunately, in their haste to leave, her parents had not noticed the tiny tin under Eve's small bed. The roof leaked in several places, and during that first lonely night, Eve was kept from sleep by the dripping of melting ice onto the stove. Her first job had been to repair the leak so that she could sleep. She never shed a tear for her parents, and the thought of trying to find them never entered her head. So she became a woodsman and taught herself to hunt the local wildlife for food. During the summer of '67 she had taken care of Skipper, a dog she had found roaming the woods around Oak Island. Skipper, in return for kindness and the sharing of her food, doted on Eve, following her everywhere.

Underneath all the dirt and oversized clothing, Eve would be deemed a pretty girl, but as she stood before Jacob and Thomsen, she looked a trifle menacing. She was alert, as was Skipper, who began to edge forward, sniffing the air.

Eve looked down at the odd collection of their meagre possessions; an embarrassingly small amount, in truth. Eve had never seen such a jumbled collection of chattels. She saw in the pile nothing that belonged to her, or her woods.

"You are a sad pair, aren't you?"

"That we are. I repeat that we just want to be on our way and mean you no harm," answered Thomsen.

"What names do you go by?"

"I am Phillip Thomsen, but people just call me Thomsen, and this is my esteemed friend, Jacob Madder." Thomsen pointed his arm towards Jacob in a flourish, as if he was introducing royalty. Jacob stood with his mouth wide open, as he too now realised that it was a young woman rather than a man who was pointing an old shotgun at them. He was also surprised that he had just found out that Thomsen actually owned a first name.

He blushed, his pale complexion flushed with the onset of embarrassment. Jacob was, after all, just a teenager, who still felt a certain awkwardness in the company of women, especially young, attractive ones. He had, however, never felt clumsy around Nancy. He'd always been comfortable with her. Perhaps this was due, in part, to having grown up together, although he preferred to think that they had held a bond that was unique and rare. The winds of change had blown steadily for a while, and his life was starting, unexpectedly, to change for the good. As he sat, looking at the beautiful Eve, he dared to think that he could once again strike up the kind of friendship he had enjoyed with Nancy.

Eve regarded the small boy in front of her. She looked him up and down, her gaze finally resting on his red face. She thought him handsome, and was drawn to his shyness. She had come across many men in Nova Scotia, and in her opinion, all of them seemed brash, uncouth, and filled with dishonourable intentions. She rarely liked men, perhaps in part because of the sudden abandonment by her father.

In Mahone Bay she would try to keep business dealings with the men of the town to a minimum, instead closing deals with the womenfolk. This, of course, was most unusual, as women were seen as homemakers, and not party to any business dealings, no matter how unimportant. A lot of the male population thought Miss Yung to be a little dour and unapproachable. They had failed – due in no small part to her dress sense – to recognise how attractive she actually was. There were others, however, who held a longing to take her into the woods to relieve her of her virginity.

"My name is Eve Yung, and this is my land. I live over yonder, and behind the furthest pine tree you can see." She pointed to the northern horizon; neither man could see any evidence of an abode through the congested pine trees. Even in winter, these evergreen trees filled the vista with their laden upper branches and dry, dusty lower limbs that knitted together, forming a dense wall. "Where are you heading for, exactly?" Eve continued.

"We don't rightly know. Our aim is to get to Halifax as soon as we can. That is, if we can find a way that doesn't require money." Jacob said, hurriedly, whilst casting a quizzical look at Thomsen.

"You both look exhausted, too tired to travel all day on a horse, I'd hazard a guess. And I don't believe you will be allowed to board the stagecoach for nothing. But I do reckon you'd scare any man or beast, looking as you do." Eve smiled at her own humour. As she spoke, she cocked open the barrel of the shotgun, cradling it over her arm in one swift movement.

Jacob and Thomsen let out audible sighs of relief. It would have just about put a cap on their time on Oak Island to be shot in the woods. Running his hands through his blond, matted hair, Jacob thought of what to say to Eve, a girl he felt drawn to, even though he knew little about her. "Do you live on your own in the woods, Eve?" he began, admonishing himself immediately at the thought that such a question would cause her to worry. However, she seldom felt vulnerable on her own patch, especially given that she was in possession of a shotgun.

"I cannot let you come to my house. You understand, don't you? I do have a hunting hide though, where we could prepare some food and let you rest before your trip." The thought suddenly occurred to her that they may be fugitives, on the run. She shook her head at once for such a stupid assumption; how could little Jacob have committed any crime? Still, she was very protective over the exact location of her home. "Come, Skipper." Her command was met with such exuberance by the big dog that it nearly knocked Thomsen over as it sped past him to its master's heel.

The hide in the woods was fairly primitive in construction, but at least afforded some shelter from the elements. Once Eve had lit the fire pit and placed a pot of water on the hefty crook suspended above the flames, the accommodation was more cheery. Two benches sat either side of the fire, which could presumably be used as beds. Eve passed both of them a large, hot cup of coffee. Bringing the drink to his lips, Jacob was relieved that her caffeine drink was sweet and slightly fruity, not at all bitter, unlike the dirty brew that Thomsen had prepared the day before. For his part, Thomsen now longed for the hipflask that Abe Riggins always carried. The rum would go very nicely with the hot beverage that his hands now clasped. But that flask was buried deep within the money pit. Thomsen thought it ironic that, perhaps, years from now, another treasure seeker would happen upon the trusty vessel that housed Abe's liquor.

As they sat in conversation, steam rose from both the cups and their breath. It had begun to snow heavily, and the branches of the trees were now covered in a white cloak. Jacob thought it looked beautiful; on Sable there were not so many trees, apart from a small wood on the western shore. As he gazed out, peering through the floating crystals, for the first time in a long time he felt relaxed. He also liked

Eve's company; she was both charming and charismatic. She openly told him about her parents and how, as a young girl, she had been able to remain alone in such a deserted and harsh landscape.

Thomsen had fallen asleep, and the sound of his snoring caused the young pair to giggle uncontrollably.

"So tell me again, Jacob, why do you need to get to Halifax?" Eve edged closer to him as she spoke. She was so close that he was intoxicated by her smell. Expecting her scent to be of wood and dirt, it was a pleasant surprise that odours of jasmine and vanilla seemed to hang in the air around her.

Jacob recounted, carefully and without emotion, all the events of the previous few days. He left no detail out, not even his supposed crime. He felt it was somehow important to tell this stranger everything, no matter how dire. As he spoke, he paid close attention to Eve, trying to gauge from her expression any sign of disgust or loathing. He knew though, in his heart, that the girl in front of him would not judge him like others may. He had found a kindred spirit. Someone like himself, who had been left abandoned by circumstance and, above all else, would not leap to any wild conclusions.

Eve Yung listened intently. Although horrified that a girl just like her was killed so brutally, she knew that the boy before her could not have committed such a heinous crime. It didn't make sense for anyone to hurt someone they patently cared about.

"My gut feeling is that I need to speak to Father Laybolt in Halifax. He will be able to understand, and counsel me on what is best. I have faith that he will guide me, even though I have never met him. That is why I need to go to the capital."

"Why are you so certain that Father Laybolt – a man you have never met – will be able to help you?"

"What else am I to do? I cannot return to Sable until the truth is out. Whatever happened that afternoon, I must find out why Nancy died, and I must not be afraid to hide the truth if it turns out that my hands played any part, significant or not."

Considering what he had been through, Eve was amazed at Jacob's maturity. In truth, inside, he was a jabbering wreck. Only Thomsen's influence had steadied him, enabled him to tell his tale.

Skipper, who was asleep beside Thomsen, let off a great sigh, then started dream-walking, his large, bear-like paws prancing in a staccato motion, as in his mind he ran along the shoreline, chasing shadows and dried seaweed blown by the wind. Eve and Jacob laughed again, and as their eyes met they both smiled.

"What date is this?" said Jacob.

"It is the twenty-eighth of October. Why do you ask?"

"Because the twenty-ninth is my birthday. I had almost forgotten that tomorrow, I reach the grand old age of seventeen. Although I don't feel like marking the day in any way, celebrating, when deep down I feel so dark. You know, Eve, before Nancy died, my heart was light."

"Well, happy birthday for tomorrow, Mr Madder. Don't be too hard on yourself, young man!" She waggled a finger, and as she spoke, a large grin filled her face. "I may bake you a cake if you are lucky!" She leaned over to Jacob and planted a warm kiss on his cheek. "Well, it's settled, you cannot leave tomorrow, you must stay another night and we can celebrate, and who knows, Thomsen may stay awake."

A strange sensation flooded Jacob's body, and he liked it. He was in no mood to celebrate anything, yet he would not object to spending more time around Eve. Guilt engulfed him. He was holding back tears. The remorse was caused by his wanting to cry; not for others, but for himself. Surely, that was wrong? Embarrassed, his gaze fell toward his boots; he was horrified to see that he had gained an erection. He hoped that Eve had not noticed, but the deepening redness of his complexion gave away his perhaps not-so-secret desire.

"I will leave you now. Get some rest, Jacob, you need it." As she spoke, she stood up, clicking her fingers, upon which her dog dutifully followed her. Jacob watched her until she had blended into the scenery and disappeared into the night. He then looked at the fire, and the dancing flames began to make his eyes heavy. He slowly lay down on the bench, crossing his arms to keep the rough-haired blanket Eve had left him close to his body and fell asleep.

Eve held a major role in Jacob's dreams that night, and he woke wondering if they were destined to be more than friends.

Eve was tending the fire. It was cold, and Skipper was playfully prancing in the deep snow, as if chasing an unseen prey.

"Morning, men. How did you sleep? I hope you were able to get a little rest. Coffee will be ready in a minute, and I have brought some biscuits for breakfast. There's more snow coming later, I can feel it." Eve seemed full of life, unlike the men, who were groggy and unfocused. Jacob looked like a small forest creature; his hair stuck up on one side and stuck to his face on the other.

Skipper rushed over to Thomsen, who, in a state between sleep and wakefulness, seemed frightened of him. Perhaps because, from his lying down position, the dog was practically the size of a donkey, and from such an angle his teeth were like big, white daggers. Skipper was not interested in biting anyone on this occasion, and seemed more concerned with trying to lick Thomsen's face. Such was the dog's fervour for washing Thomsen that he literally climbed on top of the startled sailor.

Jacob and Eve burst out laughing at the same time. "I think my dog has a thing for you, Thomsen. Either that or you've still got the remnants of your supper about your mouth! Leave him alone, Skipper."

18

The Menace of a Stranger Who Wasn't a Stranger

MAHONE BAY WAS A TOWN BUILT on the thriving activities of both lumber and fishing. It was inhabited by a hardworking, largely informal population, who, thanks to working so hard, had little time for dalliances with strangers. Three churches dominated the curved bay, while cape-style houses and large, red-painted boat-building barns dotted the coastline. The main thoroughfare ran parallel to the inlet. It was continually used by horse-drawn vehicles both domestic and industrial, and as such was uneven and rutted.

It was Friday, just after nine in the morning. It had snowed again, all night. A thick fog shrouded the town, which was under a carpet of snow as Eli James wandered along Main Street. The crunching of new snow amused him as he recalled a distant memory of making snow angels with Nancy and Jacob.

He wore a deep red scarf that he had found in the carriage which had brought him from Lunenburg. The muffler had a strange smell that was not altogether unpleasant. Eli took in deep snorts of the aroma as he proceeded towards the centre of town.

The fog was so thick that he could not see more than twenty paces ahead. Full tide meant that to his right-hand side he could hear the gentle lapping of the water against the rocky shoreline. Up ahead, he could make out the sounds of a heated argument. He strode on with a marginally quicker step.

"Forty dollars for that! You're a robbing bastard, Jack Wills. I should have known better than to enter into business with you." A tall, thin man was wagging his finger directly into the face of a much smaller, younger man, presumably the aforementioned Jack Wills.

"How was I to know that the things were diseased?" Wills was looking down at a wooden cage, which housed six dead chickens. "They were alright when I gave 'em you, flapping about, making all sorts of noise they was."

"I want my money back, now, or else I will sort you out, good and proper, do you understand?"

"Just give Linton his money back, and be on your way," said a young woman who had just arrived - Eve, though Eli didn't know it. "It gets tedious when you two argue."

"That's right, Jack, you listen to Eve."

Wills took off his left boot, driving his arm deep into it. His hand returned, clutching a crumpled wad of dollar bills. "Five, ten, twenty, thirty and forty." He slammed the bills into the tall man's outstretched palm. "I have some pigs back home if you're interested?"

The tall man and Eve Yung laughed out loud, as Jack Wills, shoulders slumped, muttering about what he would say to Mrs Wills, wandered off into the mist.

"Now, Eve, what have you got for me today? Wooden pegs, perhaps?"

The young woman began the barter with the three men that gathered around her. It was hard to make out facial features, but there was no mistaking that beneath all the dirt and dust Eve was an attractive girl. The men towered above her, yet she seemed to hold sway over them, and they hung on her every word.

Eli was still loitering on the fringes of the small group. He was cautiously waiting for the right moment to start his enquiries. After the cool reception he had encountered in Lunenburg, he wanted to choose the right person to talk to. His eyes met Eve's for a moment as she continued to talk, seemingly aware that she was the centre of attention.

"Linton, you would not believe what's happened. Another couple of treasure hunters walked off Oak Island into my woods three nights ago."

"More fools arriving at your place every month, so no, I am not surprised at anything you tell me, Eve."

"I do know only one of them seemed after the treasure. The other told me an amazing tale. One that involved the murder of a girl on Sable Island!" Eve knew Linton liked a tale. He would be straight home to tell his wife, and before long, the whole town would know.

Eli's attention was suddenly grabbed, as if in a vice. He

edged forward, tilting his whole body as he spoke.

"Hello there, I am from Sable, and know of the events surrounding the unfortunate death of Nancy Haas." He had now crept forward so much that he found himself right in the middle of the group. "I have come over from the island to find my best friend, Jacob Madder, who everyone thought perished."

"I can tell you that Jacob is well and truly alive." Eve said, looking squarely into Eli's eyes. She felt a sense of unease as she looked at this other boy from Sable Island. With Jacob, she felt comfortable, but now she became nervous and agitated, as if she had an irritating itch. She wished that she had kept silent about her visitors, but she was a well-mannered girl, and would show a level of politeness. After all, if this was Jacob's best friend, he couldn't be all that bad, could he?

The news was both a shock and relief to Eli, who now, for the first time since Nancy's death, felt a return of control to the situation. It was a feeling he was used to, a feeling he expected to feel. If he could find Jacob, he knew what he had to do. It would not be pleasant, yet needs must. "Are you totally sure that it was Jacob you met?" he asked.

"Do you take me for a liar?" Eve was now really annoyed, and her initial suspicions about Eli resurfaced.

"I can tell you, young man, that Eve Yung never speaks without it being the truth," Linton interjected, making sure that his posture was erect as he spoke, so that he was taller than Eli.

"Sorry to cause offense, I just needed to be sure that it was Jacob. All of us on the island thought him drowned. Do you have any idea where he was heading?"

"I may have an idea." Eve was deliberately being careful with her choice of words. Something told her she could not trust this stranger.

"I wonder, then, if it would be possible to discuss this matter further, elsewhere?" Eli was quite clearly trying hard to remain patient. His eyes, however, told a different story, as they glared at Eve.

"There is a place up there, by the main loading dock, where we can get a hot drink. We can talk about Jacob, but first I have to finish my business here. If you walk up there and go to the small red hut on your left, and say Eve has sent you, they will let you wait. I will come as soon as I can." Eve knew that the meetinghouse would be crowded today so she would not be alone with Eli. She also wanted to have a little time to think about what she should say.

Without saying a word, Eli left, and trudged up Main Street just as Eve had instructed.

"Boy, he's a bit serious," muttered Linton. "I believe all those who live on that island are a bit queer, though especially when there's been murdering." Linton shook his head. He had known quite a few who had hailed from Sable or Ironbound, and all were a bit odd in one way or another.

Stirring his sweet tea rhythmically, Eli frowned, staring down at the stone mug, not wanting to catch the eye of anyone. He was in no mood for idle banter. The other men kept their distance, sensing correctly that he was angry and should not be approached. Who was this girl that told him what to do? Slumping forward, he covered his face with his hands. Patience was not one of his strongest attributes and the longer she took, the angrier he would become. Years of excoriating everyone he met instilled a hostile underbelly in his thoughts.

The rickety front door flew open, and she entered to a volley of welcomes and jibes from the gathered crowd. There were four small tables, each occupied by three men apart from the table in the corner, where Eli sat, alone with his thoughts.

"Here she is, boys," said one particularly rough-looking boat-builder.

"How about you let me squeeze those tits?" shouted Josh Roberts, a gaunt man with a straggly beard and skin the colour of rust. It was often a cause of discussion as to whether his skin was naturally brown or if he just needed a good wash.

"Maybe tomorrow, Roberts, if you scrub those fish innards off your hands," Eve quipped; she was used to the coarseness of the men and had no problem putting them in their place. She quickly spotted Eli in the far corner and, pushing past the men sat at an adjacent table, headed for him. Without saying a word, Eli, using his feet, pushed the chair out. The resultant scraping noise echoed around the hut.

"So, tell me again, who are you and why are you here?"

Eve asked.

Eli was comfortable telling his tale, one that was just due south of the truth. He explained that he had arrived on the mainland with the sole intent of aiding a friend in need. He embellished his sorrow for what had happened back on Sable and told Eve that his purpose was to ensure that Jacob was not only alive but no longer on the run. There had been a mistake, and no-one suspected Jacob anymore, so it was safe to return.

Despite her suspicions, Eve felt that perhaps he was actually being sincere and only acted in the best interests of Jacob after all. She told him about Jacob's travel plans and also of his older companion.

"You may stay on my land, following in Jacob's footsteps, if you like. We must get going though as I need to drop something at Martin's River and want to get home before dark."

Draining the last of his tea, Eli collected the small bag of belongings at his feet and followed Eve outside. Taking into account the drop-off at Martin's River, the journey home took just shy of three hours. One hundred and eighty minutes of near silence.

The cart slowed to a stop outside the wood store, just at the edge of the woods. Eve alighted in one slick movement, landing firmly on the bed of snow. Behind them, the tracks they had just made could clearly be seen. Eli brushed off the day's dirt, tightened the red scarf still tied firmly around his neck, and climbed down. The horse nudged him as he reached the ground, sending him onto his backside. Eve chuckled and patted the mare tenderly on her withers. Eli rose and dug his finger deep into the horse's neck as he passed by. The horse bolted, moving away from any potential threat.

"Don't you ever touch my horse again." Eve scowled; she was angry. A single command whistle brought Skipper to her side. Eli backed away; he had never seen such a big dog. "I suggest you rest, as you will be leaving in the morning. Skipper, come," The big dog, ignoring Eli, dutifully turned and followed Eve. "Are you coming? I will show you where you can sleep tonight. Don't think of trying to follow me afterwards, though. You will get lost in these woods at night, especially now that the snow covers everything."

"I didn't mean to upset you, I'm just tired after my journey. I assure you I will be on my way first thing in the morning."

Eve left Eli at the hide, the same shelter that Jacob and Thomsen had utilised three days ago. The snow was deep on the path back to her house, and her feet sank as she moved forward. Pausing, Eve turned to take one more look at where she had left Eli, perhaps checking that his intent was to rest rather than to follow her. Moonlight flooded through the snow-laden branches of the trees. There was no movement, so she continued on her way home.

He left it a good hour before he tried to follow her. As the snow had now stopped he hoped to find her tracks with relative ease. He held the small knife that he had found stuck into the timber wall of the hide. The handle, made of ivory, was smooth through years of use, and the blade, surprisingly sharp. Eve's father had bought it twenty years ago and left it behind when he abandoned both his home and daughter. Eve never touched it and had left it protruding out of the timber frame of the shelter.

"I hope that dog is tied up," Eli said aloud as he trudged along, placing his own boots in the shallow hollows Eve had left in the snow. Passing between two large pine trees, he emerged within a large clearing. Silently, he approached the small cabin Eve called home, careful not to alert anyone or anything to his presence. The last thing he needed right now was a confrontation with a big, black hound. Smiling, as he realised that the dog was nowhere to be seen, he crouched down behind a pile of tree trunks that had been left out to season. He ran his thumb along the blade of the ivory-handled knife, as if seeking reassurance that if Skipper leapt out he had some protection.

From his hiding place, he could clearly make out Eve through the small window to the left of her scruffy front door. The mottled glass seemed to pulse, as the light from the oil lantern flickered. She had already removed her coat and was untying the ribbons that held her hair in a style more conservative than when it hung freely over her slender shoulders. As her long hair dropped forward, she reached down to splash her pretty face with water from the earthenware bowl she had filled. Now that her outer clothes were discarded, there was no hiding the heavy womanliness of her hips and breasts. Eli involuntarily let forth a small moan. Wetting his lips like a lizard testing the air before striking at an innocent prey, he felt the stirrings of arousal. Rubbing his crotch rhythmically, he sensed a tingle that he liked.

Eve, unaware she was being watched, delicately removed her pale blue cotton blouse, placing it neatly on top of the folded pile of her other clothes. It was still cold in the house, as the fire had not yielded enough heat to fill even one room. A shiver ran through her, causing her nipples to stand erect against the gossamer material of the vest she wore. Dark circles could clearly be seen, as if she wore no garment at all. She dipped a rectangular flannel into the water; wrung it out, then, lifting her right arm, she gently wiped her hollow, hairless armpit. A trickle of the warm water ran along the outline of her firm breast. Dipping the flannel back into the bowl, she squeezed out the excess liquid and reached down to clean her vagina. She clearly enjoyed the sensation, and, raising her head, she closed her eyes as she massaged herself a little harder. She was wet, and her index finger moved slowly against her clitoris. She had no mother to tell her things only a mother should. She had, years before, dealt with the shock of her first monthly period alone – she had thought, in a panic, that she was dying and had tried to stop the bleeding with a bandage.

As she stood now at the window, the ecstasy she was feeling was wonderful. Feeling slightly ashamed, she brought her finger to her lips to taste her own orgasm. She re-opened her eyes and looked out at the snow. Her skin flushed as she realised that she had thought of Jacob as she had touched herself.

Eli hadn't realised how beautiful she was. More perfect than Nancy Haas, more of a woman. He desperately wanted to touch her. The urge had returned. Her masturbation had inflamed him. Slowly, he approached the back door, pausing to recall the last time he had felt the urge and its consequences. Eve was so pretty he couldn't help himself.

19

A Familiar Face in the Doorway at St. Paul's

TO THE EYES OF ANY ISLANDER, downtown Halifax would be vastly different to Freetown on Sable Island. To the eyes of young Jacob Madder it was a world apart. It was not only the stone buildings that were prevalent in the state capital – whereas on Sable every building was made of timber – the very smell that hung in the air was different. Not the salty, fresh scent with occasional fishy hints, but a slightly heavy, industrial, metallic stench, born of shipbuilding and a larger populace. To Jacob, who had spent most of his life on a small island, the noise and bustle were both intoxicating and frightening. He had only been to the city once before, as a very young boy, accompanying his parents as they went about their business.

Back then, everything had been covered in a shroud of thick cloud, and a constant drizzle had enveloped the harbour. They had disembarked from the carriage just in front of the citadel and had a bird's eye view of the waterfront. There is something magical to a young boy about a first glimpse of any metropolis. Looking back,

Jacob was reminded of his own memory as if it were another lifetime, another boy holding his father's hand as they looked at the same image he now gazed upon. He wondered if he had actually been happy as that six-year-old, or had the passage of time softened his recollections? Had he forgotten the welts from the belt?

"Are you alright, Jacob?" Thomsen was concerned at the grave expression that washed over his companion's features. It was a look he had never seen on Jacob's youthful face.

"Sorry, yes, I'm fine. Don't worry about me, Thomsen, I just hail from a background of high-quality guilt. There really is no need for us to dwell further on my own self-pity. We must find the Reverend Cole's friend, Father Laybolt, I am convinced he will be able to help us." Jacob once again recalled – as he had discussed with Eve – Nancy's father talking very fondly of a religious colleague from Halifax. This was the aforementioned Father Laybolt, whom Cole had first met when he was a young, impressionable religious scholar. Born from very different backgrounds, it was strange – given the different paths of faith and the difference in age – that they remained good friends despite the distance between them.

"How do we find him? There must be at least fifty churches in this city," Thomsen wondered, as he looked out over the great conurbation.

"I suppose we should start with that one and just ask. Surely, someone will know of him or, at the very least, guide us to where we should direct our enquiries." Jacob pointed to a small spire in the distance and set off, safe in the knowledge that his friend would follow.

Father Laybolt was a devout follower of the Anglican Church who had spent his life anchored in worship. He always welcomed people to his services no matter what religious denomination they followed. Cole had met Laybolt by chance, and the two had formed a friendship. Indeed, Cole had chosen Father Laybolt as a witness when he married Sophia.

Some in his congregation considered his beliefs too radical, due in part to these people being typically conservative and, above all, suspicious of strangers. Others, however, thought it refreshing to have a minister who concerned himself with pure devotion to God rather than highlighting the differences between one faith and another. Stoic by nature, he was a man you could depend upon. Laybolt was slight of stature, with a mop of golden hair flowing across an angular face. His eyes of deepest green always focused keenly on whoever met him. It was said that Father Laybolt was a strong man, perhaps not of body but most definitely of mind. He had been the pastor at St Paul's in Halifax for ten years. A very popular minister, he was especially liked by the patrons of the Press Gang restaurant some forty paces from the church's front door. He was known to sit at table twenty-two most Wednesday and Friday evenings after prayer, where, after little encouragement, he would knock out a few tunes on the in-house piano. The impromptu sing-alongs were always well-received, and the restaurant was always busy when the father played.

Jacob and Thomsen were informed, after minimal enquiry, as to the whereabouts of the father and arrived at St. Paul's around lunchtime. The corner position of the building was well thought-out, in that it commanded views of both Argyle and Barrington Street intersections. Stood in the doorway, one would be able to survey a wide panorama. Barrington Street in particular housed many historic properties, including the aforementioned watering hole Father Laybolt favoured.

The heavy wooden door groaned as Jacob pushed it open. "Hello?" His voice reverberated in the empty vestibule. He took time to look at a row of old Bibles stacked ready to be handed to an eager congregation as they entered the service. Several of the books needed repair, damaged by those that nervously thumbed them, whilst others gripped them as if their lives depended on keeping a firm grasp of the Good Book. It was comforting to Jacob to see that they were well-used, suggesting an above average attendance.

"Hello, Father Laybolt," he shouted again, as he slowly shuffled forward. Thomsen, meanwhile, had quickly moved to the far side of the large nave and, pausing at the chancel, was studying the ornate altar a few feet ahead of him. He thought of Riggins and how, if he had lived, and been in Thomsen's shoes, he may have made off with the shiny candlesticks and crucifixes. Riggins would have feared no wrath of God; he would have believed it his right to put the trinkets in his pockets.

A loud clunk of brass keys turning in a hidden doorway stopped them both in their tracks. In unison, they looked up like naughty schoolchildren caught in the act of doing something mischievous.

"Who's there?" enquired Laybolt, his golden hair shimmering in the flickering light of the candle he needed when travelling the dark recesses of the church. "Can I help you?"

"We are friends of Cole Haas, father," Jacob said, stepping forward from behind the row of oak pews. He hoped this would allay any fears the preacher would have about his unexpected visitors.

"Cole, you say? Cole Haas, a very good man. Oh good, welcome, welcome to my humble place of worship. Welcome to St. Paul's."

Looking to all four corners of the church, Jacob thought it far from humble. He had rarely seen such beauty made from stone and wood. Sure, his dory was hand-crafted to an exquisite finish, but it paled in comparison to the quality of the craftsmanship prevalent inside St Paul's. It must have taken many men many hours to complete.

"My name is Jacob Madder, and this is my good friend, Thomsen. I have travelled here from Sable Island and I have grave news of your friend. Well, of his daughter, Nancy. Is there somewhere we can talk?"

"Yes, of course, but I have to deliver some supplies to

Halifax Common and I am dreadfully late already."

"I can go on your behalf," offered Thomsen, who had left the nave. "Jacob can then tell you about Cole and why we sought you out."

"That's very kind. Follow me and I'll show you what needs taking.

Thomsen put on his overcoat quickly, in preparation for leaving. It mattered little that he would be heading beyond the citadel, to a place he didn't know. Quite frankly, he was just relieved to be leaving the church. Less comfortable than Jacob in the company of religious types or the educated, Thomsen was more than happy to have volunteered to go. He and Father Laybolt left together, heading for the priest's private quarters to collect the box of food vouchers and a few tins of canned fish.

Jacob was left alone with only the assorted bibles and prayer books for company. He decided to sit on one of the pews directly in front of the pulpit, imagining Cole Haas towering above the congregation, delivering a powerful message of hope. Oh, how he longed for things to be as they once were. He closed his eyes and listened to the creaking of the building, just making out the familiar noise of horse-drawn carts passing by on Barrington Street.

The nefarious Eli leaned forward in the pew directly behind Jacob's. How long had he been sat in the shadows?

"Jacob, I've been dying to tell you something," he whispered. Immediately, Jacob recognised his friend's voice. He sat up, turning to look behind him to confirm his belief. A smile began to spread over his face; his friend had come to help him. Perhaps things were about to take a turn for the better?

"Don't look at me!" Eli yelled, taking Jacob aback . "You must not look at me until I have said what has to be said. I believe that I am both more resourceful and more cunning than you. I always have been. You know they think it was you who killed Nancy, don't you? They are fools, they don't even suspect that it was I who was responsible."

Jacob breathed in, deep and slow. His pulse had risen and he began to tremble; it was now confirmed that he was not, after all, culpable in Nancy's death. He could hardly believe what he was hearing; he was angry that he had ever felt guilty, and rage rose inside him, replacing the fear. He clenched his teeth and pursed his lips as Eli – seemingly gloating about his actions – continued.

"I couldn't help myself. She started screaming and shouting. All I wanted was to touch her, to smell her; she always encouraged me and then rejected me. That wasn't right, if only she had been a good girl and let me feel her, none of it would have happened."

"There is no excuse for what you have done, Eli."

"Maybe. But the girl in the woods did the same, showing me things, egging me on. I know you liked her, Jacob, she told me so and you just couldn't have her, not before me."

"Eve – you haven't harmed her, please tell me you're just trying to hurt me. I will kill you myself if..." Jacob stood up, clenching both fists as he turned to face his one-time friend.

"Oh, Jacob, you are so tough. Have your misadventures out at sea transformed you? You're forgetting how much stronger I am than you. I have always been. Maybe you should call into her little house in the woods. She waits for you, Jacob, she isn't going anywhere. You're such a little turd, my old friend." Eli grabbed Jacob's arm, twisting it as he squeezed. Jacob yelped, as much out of shock as pain.

Father Laybolt, alerted to the peril of his young visitor, ran between the pews to the left of where Eli had hold of Jacob's arm. "Let him go, now, whoever you are!"

"Who the hell are you?" Eli sneered.

"I am someone you would be well-advised to listen to," Laybolt said as he approached, making himself as non-confrontational as possible by holding his arms out, palms up, holding nothing. Eli let go of Jacob and, as he turned, slipped his hand into one of the deep pockets of his overcoat. Unknown to Father Laybolt, he held a firm grip on the dagger he had collected at Eve's shelter. He was poised, coiled like a snake ready to attack.

Lurching forward, he thrust the small blade deep into the priest's stomach. Once again he had attacked, without thought, another minister, this time with a blade rather than cruel words. Retrieving the weapon from the wound, he headed for the main exit without pause. The father, caught unaware by such a barbaric act, fell to his knees, clutching his abdomen. Jacob instinctively bent down to help the poor cleric rather than giving chase.

Looking up briefly, Jacob caught just a parting glimpse of Eli's face before the main door closed. At that moment, Eli looked frightened – frightened of what? It certainly wasn't that he feared being caught. No, Jacob had seen a greater anxiety on his face – that he had let go of his past, and there would be no going back to the simpler life he had led on Sable Island. Eli was incapable of concealing such a deep-rooted fear from someone who had known him all of his life. His was not the familiar face in the doorway Jacob had known; his was the face of a killer.

20

The Ship Sails

IT HAD SNOWED ALL NIGHT, AND from where Jacob was standing in front of St Paul's, he could see a fresh layer of white covering the gravestones like a giant tarpaulin. Inside, Father Laybolt sat slumped against the east wall. He felt as if he had witnessed true evil, perhaps even been in the presence of a disciple of Satan himself. Gaunt and pale, he had not slept since the event. His wound was in need of urgent medical attention, yet he refused to leave the church.

Thomsen had returned to find chaos. He was angry that he had not been present to deal with Eli. After applying a bandage to the father, he had gone in search of a doctor.

The revelations Eli had made the previous evening still hung in the air, heavy and oppressive. Seldom in his life had Jacob felt so helpless. Seldom had he felt so sad. He felt as if the queen of broken hearts had arrived to gloat at his misfortune. A supposed friend had robbed him of his only chance of true love, in the cruellest of ways.

He tried not to dwell further on his personal loss. He knew it was important that he gathered his thoughts and carried on. It was up to him, and him alone, to ensure Nancy and Eve's killer was brought to justice. In the case of the former, it was critical that everyone knew that he, Jacob, had not been responsible for her death. Revenge was an emotion that could stir the blood within any man. Nevertheless, it had to be controlled. Certainly, this could not be managed through age and experience, but rather by pure self-control. Jacob also hoped that Father Laybolt would make a full recovery and felt guilty – the priest would not have been harmed if he had not tried to protect him.

Jacob had to find Eli. He decided to spend the whole day making enquiries in all parts of the city. Father Laybolt was decidedly against such a plan and had tried to persuade him to go directly to the constable.

"Thomsen will speak to the constable, I promise you," said Jacob. "When he has returned with a doctor to assist you, he will see to it. Don't fret about me. Tell Thomsen that I have left and will see him later, when I have found Eli James."

"Be very careful, Jacob. That young man has been touched by something that we cannot understand. Something that conceives he is powerful, and that is dangerous. Promise me you will not confront him without help."

"Yes, father, I will be careful, just concentrate on getting your injury seen to. I will return soon."

Jacob was more determined than ever and set off into the cold morning confident that fate would again deliver him the opportunity to get close to Eli.

Stepping from the shadow cast by the steeple of the church on Barrington Street, he quickly ate up the paving stones. Avoiding eye contact with absolutely everyone, he turned into Sackville Street and headed for the waterfront. An old lady shouted as he passed, seeking any loose change, and, out of character, he completely ignored her. This act caused her to shout a profanity, before resuming her slow trundle along the sidewalk. The sun was trying its best to break through heavy cloud cover. It was bitterly cold travelling in the shadows of the tall granite buildings. The wind rushed from the bay as if pushed up a gigantic funnel. Jacob pulled his coat tighter as he marched on. His boots were now two-toned, as the damp snow had begun to seep into the leather. The hint of heat given off from the intermittent sun had started a slow thaw. Grubby piles of slush stood dwindling at the side of the road as Jacob picked his way towards the berth that was temporary home to a large steamship.

At the waterfront, a small crowd had gathered to see the ship off. From some distance, Jacob estimated that it wouldn't be long before she sailed. Dark smoke had begun to drift from the main funnel into the greying sky, and there were already two barges alongside, ready to ease her from the manmade dock into open water.

A loud foghorn signalled her departure. Jacob was now rushing through the throng, trying to take in the sea of faces as he passed. He was convinced that Eli would be drawn to the waterfront and perhaps an escape from

Canada altogether. Instinct led him forward, yet there was still no sign of Eli.

Still he pressed on, arriving at the berth vacated by the great ship to find tearful onlookers mournfully waving as the ship entered the main channel leading out to open water. On board, a scattering of brave passengers stood against the rail and the biting cold to wave their white handkerchiefs. They knew it would be some time before they saw these shores again. The ship had sailed.

In reality, none would see any shore again. The ship floundered in mysterious circumstances nine days into her voyage. Not one soul survived the tragedy, the only evidence coming weeks later, when a stone bottle was discovered containing a strange message on a screwed-up piece of paper.

'We are fast settling. We have lost four of our men overboard, a further three have died. Our lives are in great danger. The ship is on fire and we are hurrying all passengers to the bows. Our propeller is broken, and we are at the entire mercy of the waves. God help us.

Whoever finds this bottle will do a great kindness in forwarding it to – W. Inman, Water Street, Liverpool'

Many thought the note a hoax as it was signed by names that were neither on the passenger list nor the articles of agreement. The ship was never found, and the Inman Line changed its policy concerning recording passengers as a result of the tragedy. In future the recording of actual passengers by most commercial shipping lines was taken far more seriously. Indeed it was often the case that you would not be allowed to board or disembark unless you had either a ticket to travel or a specific day-pass which enabled you to say farewell to loved ones.

Jacob frantically tried to find out if it would be possible to be taken to the ship by one of the smaller vessels idly sat tethered to the main dock. He was met with a flurry of shaking heads, confirming that he had arrived too late. Heavy-hearted, he trudged off to find a representative of the Inman Shipping Company.

21

Back on Sable

TOM MADDER WAS AWOKEN BY AN urgent need to urinate. For the past hour, he had unconsciously felt this way. The anvil-like weight pressing down on his bladder had made him uncomfortable, yet he had remained cocooned in the thick blankets that covered the large oak bed he lay upon. He had not moved for two days, and the chamber-pot beneath him was ripe and overdue attention.

The previous day, he had been awakened by a sound. At least, he thought it was a sound, a crunching sound, like sticky snow underfoot in the silence which blanketed Sable when the fishermen rested. He listened again, but the only noise he could hear was the distant cry of the gulls in the harbour. He returned to his melancholic state, drifting from reality to dream and back again.

It was Christmas, yet he was in no mood to be part of any festivities or celebrations. The sound of the occasional passer-by – no doubt on a quest to either visit a neighbour or prepare for a visitation themselves – failed to stir him. They must have known he was inside, yet quickened their steps as they passed the Madder residence.

Sadness and regret had engulfed the big man. He knew that there were few who liked him, few who cared that he survived. Not one islander had knocked on his door since he had returned. He had not eaten, yet was not hungry. The winter weather threw itself against the timber shingles, tapping rhythmically as the flakes of crystalline water fell from the darkened sky. Snow had accumulated above the scruffy shrubs that his wife had once tended. They resembled a line of small ghosts in an orderly queue to enter the house.

The loss of his son was simply too hard to bear. Jacob had been his constant, the one thing he could rely on. Why then had he rarely shown his only son kindness? As he lay, unwilling to get up and start again, he searched his memory for just one good recollection, one happy memory concerning his time with Jacob. None sprang to his mind, only all the times he had chastised his son for simply being a child. It is a poor father who only dwells on a child's shortcomings and never praises a triumph, even the insignificant ones. Oh, how he wished he could go back. His late wife always told him he would one day regret his actions. He was too pig-headed to listen. His was a life full of regret.

Feeling lower than ever, he cast his attention to the physical wounds that he knew would never fully heal. His body was scarred. Particularly his hand, where the giant seabird had sustained itself by feeding on the open cut he had suffered when the Saxby Gale first hit.

A rapping on the front door interrupted his malaise. He should simply ignore it, he thought. Pulling the bed sheets above his head, he turned over, closing his eyes, not for sleep but to hide. He thought of a great bear hibernating each winter, away from the world in a den. He had once seen one close up, on a trip to Manitoba.

The banging on his front door continued, relentlessly. It wasn't that he was particularly worried about ignoring anyone, more that he desired the noise to stop that finally forced Tom from his bed. He shuffled to the window, from where he would be able to see exactly who was disturbing this latest bout of self-pity. He was surprised to see Lisbeth James below, patiently knocking on the wooden door with the handle of her umbrella. Unlatching the bedroom window, Tom leaned out and, after a short coughing fit, issued instructions to his visitor. "There's a key under the black stone, let yourself in and I will be down presently."

"Unbelievable," he muttered to himself as he paused at the small smoky mirror – God he looked a mess, and probably smelt one too. And he wasn't about to put on his pants for no-one. Anyhow, he expected the visit to be brief, and then he could return to his slumber in peace.

Lisbeth sat nervously on a small wooden chair in Tom's kitchen. She had placed a panful of stew on the table and was picking at a loose thumbnail with her index finger.

"So what brings you to my house? Shouldn't you be at home, looking after Robert?" Tom said, pulling up the chair directly opposite his guest.

"I was worried about you, Tom. I knew you wouldn't be eating and looking after yourself, so I made you some stew," Lisbeth said, as compassionately as she could manage. Tom had always had a strange relationship with Lisbeth. They were both forthright and opinionated and as such had an understanding which allowed them to tolerate each other. Politeness was maintained in public, but otherwise, caustic exchanges or complete ignorance were employed. It was natural, then, that Tom treated this apparent act of kindness with a modicum of suspicion.

"I know we have not always got along, Tom, but what happened to Nancy has made me think we should put all our differences aside and support each other. Robert thinks the same as I. He does care for you. You know that, don't you?"

"Rubbish, Lisbeth. You're here to delight in my circumstance, I know it."

"No, you're wrong. Come on, have some food, you definitely look as though a hearty meal would do you some good."

Tom shifted uneasily. He remained sceptical of Lisbeth's apparent friendliness. Mind you, the stew smelled wonderful, and he suddenly became aware that he was quite hungry. He ate straight from the pan at the rate of a starving dog.

"So, how is Robert?" he said between mouthfuls.

Lisbeth, with most unnatural attention, was eyeing his every move as he devoured the food she had brought. She thought of a hog; a big, fat pig. If he in turn had studied her facial expressions, he would have noticed the disdain she was painfully trying to hide.

"Good, isn't it? And Robert is fine, considering. Thanks for asking." In response, Tom let out a great belch, then wiped the corners of his mouth with the sleeve of his dirty nightshirt. That was it! She couldn't stand to be in this house any longer. She stood up, brushed the front of her blue pinafore and put on her black overcoat. "You can have the pot, Tom, I don't want it now. I will see myself out and tell Robert you asked about him. Goodbye, Tom Madder, and Merry Christmas to you." She closed the front door and was gone.

Tom sat, mouth agape, speechless. There had been a certain finality in her departure, a weirdness in her words that he couldn't quite put his finger on. She had at least brought him a grand meal, but had then left without wanting her stewpot. It was odd, but then again 'odd' was not out of place when sitting at a table with Lisbeth James. He returned to his bed, leaving the dirty pot at the table.

It was only four hours later when the pain began. A searing pain across his midriff as well as an itching sensation, as if his skin was covered in ants. Death loitered in every corner of the house, ready to engulf Tom and remove him from this world. The toxins had started their journey from blood stream to organs, and it would only be a few more hours until the foreign ingredient did its job.

On her way back to the lighthouse, Lisbeth James wore

a knowing smile. She knew no-one would suspect that it was her gift that had killed someone. Someone who would have ultimately threatened her dear son, and she would not allow that to happen. They would assume that he had died as a result of both a broken body and a wretched state of mind. And certainly, there would not be one person that would question the missing vile of arsenic commonly used to control the vermin that waged a constant battle beneath the lighthouse. The stock had been purchased in bulk and distributed amongst the many Atlantic lighthouses long before either the 1851 sale of arsenic act or the potentially incriminating poison book.

She hurried along, knowing that Robert would soon be demanding his festive luncheon. One down, one to go was all she thought as she strode on, not caring that the wind had burnt her face.

22

Boarding the Ship to Liverpool

THE 'CITY OF BOSTON' HAD ARRIVED in port unexpectedly. She had left New York bound for Liverpool in the old world. Captain Halcrow, who commanded the vessel, was already in poor spirits. His impressive, well-groomed whiskers gave him an air of authority normally associated with heads at scholastic academies rather than sailors. He was famed for always ensuring that his portmanteau was well-stocked with salt beef and other dried food. He seldom trusted the ship's cookie and was fanatical in ensuring his digestive wellbeing.

The ship's owners had decided to increase the profitability of the voyage by an extra stop in Nova Scotia. The few passengers – who had each paid handsomely for the shorter journey – had been a constant source of agitation to the ship's crew with their continuous grumblings about the state of their accommodation. Fortunately, all were now off the ship. Halcrow hoped that the few passengers they were collecting in Halifax would be more tolerant on the twelve-day crossing.

The port labourers had not expected the ship to arrive

at all; no word had been sent. No notice or docket was to be seen. The disgruntled workforce, who were both treated and recompensed poorly, left the taverns on the promise of a few dollars in return for some extra work. Some had even already spent their prospective earnings on alcohol and prostitutes. Such was the predisposition of these men.

Eli, having fled from St Paul's, continued along Barrington Street, constantly looking this way and that in case he was being followed. His mind was racing, searching for options; he spied the large steamship 'The City of Boston' in berth in the main harbour. Guessing from the sheer size of the vessel, he decided it would be bound for overseas. He formulated his plan on the short journey down to the docks. He knew it was only a matter of time before he would be sought for stabbing the man inside the church, and that investigation could lead to the truth about the murders of Nancy and Eve. The thought of leaving Canada altogether was daunting to such a young man, yet he had little option. He would not survive in prison, let alone cope with the shame he would bring on his family.

Confusion and chaos abounded, and after some negotiation with a surly man in the ticket booth, he was able to secure the last third-class ticket available. It was explained to him that as he was a last minute passenger; he would have to fill out the necessary documents on-board. He thought of using a different name, although he had no papers to support such a deception. He then considered how much money would be required to bribe the purser.

If, however, the purser was an honest man, he could be arrested.

Something suddenly leapt into his mind. His mother, who often talked to her only son rather than her husband, had made mention of a brother in Yarmouth. When her father had died he had left the profits of his not-inconsiderable talents as a gambler and thief in eight flour tins. They were each stuffed with cash and other valuables. Eli's uncle, Bradley, had immediately taken charge of all the tins. This had caused a vast rift between Bradley and Eli's mother, and they hadn't spoken to each other since. It was generally accepted, in the early part of the nineteenth century, that the oldest male heir would assume control of such heirlooms beyond question.

Twenty years had now passed, and even though Eli's mother had a new life on Sable Island, her resentment had grown. The last she had heard of her brother was that he had followed in her father's footsteps and become a drunk. Amazingly, Bradley had managed to hold onto a small percentage of her father's fortune, although she could not guess how much had actually survived his frivolous ways. She presumed he had hidden the remaining tin or tins somewhere in the family house on Main Street, Yarmouth.

Eli thought that if he could somehow deceive people into thinking he had absconded overseas, he could then travel to Yarmouth to seek his uncle and get hold of his mother's inheritance.

As the ship was readied for departure, the deck was

awash with people. To the inexperienced eye it seemed that chaos ensued, passengers, sailors, and weeping relatives saying goodbye to friends and family rushing this way and that. On the starboard upper deck, Eli ghosted through the throng. One hand firmly gripped the last of his mother's money – the cash he had stolen – while he used the other as a buffer against his fellow journeymen. He was sure he would not be followed; he had taken a chance by exposing his guilt to those inside St Paul's. He was angry that he had used a considerable slice of his cash to pay for passage, but it was vital that his name appeared on the manifest carried about the deck by the ship's pursers. A copy of the manifest would be left, often incomplete, with the Harbour Master. Eli's name would be noted on the part-filled document as a steerage passenger, bound for England.

Naturally, he had lied about his place of birth, age, profession, and the address of his parents. Indeed, the only truth on his form, apart from his name, was his height and hair colour. Eli looked older than his seventeen years, so the young official was easy to deceive. The extra five dollars given to the blond-haired purser certainly aided the deception.

His decision to jump ship and flee had been supported when he had personally examined steerage. It was damp, dark, and overcrowded deep in the bowels of the steamship. The food crate that the Inman Line had provided for the lower-class passengers to cook was overrun with rodents.

Eli knew exactly what he must do next. He had to leave

the province as soon as possible. The window to travel anonymously would be small. He had to make that one last stop in Yarmouth and then cross the Bay of Fundy and on to America, where he could disappear armed with money enough to start a new life.

There were things he would long for when he finally left Nova Scotia. He would similarly miss certain of the quirky ways of those who lived on Sable Island. He just didn't know it yet. Young people often left the quieter places of this world in search of fortune or excitement, often returning years later, as if family ties had only given them temporary leave to try something else in another place.

It was imperative that he made his escape undetected. Like a feral cat, he drifted into the shadows of the steamship. Pulling the collar of his dark grey overcoat up, and tying the red scarf he had gained en route to Mahone Bay firmly around his lower jaw, he returned to the busy throng on main deck. His hope was that he would leave the boat unnoticed, as if he were just there seeing off a loved one.

"Hey, you there!" rang a booming voice above the noise of the crowd.

'Just ignore it; it's not you they seek,' he thought as he strode on, trying to blend into the crowd.

"You with the red scarf, wait!" A rather large Haligonian man shouted again, parting the people between them in the process. They were all looking directly at him. The game was up, and he had been found out. Eli slowly turned to face the seaman, who wasn't actually a sailor but rather an employee of the shipping line based in the port, all the while searching for any possible escape.

"You dropped this." The purser held up the small parchment paper package containing all of Eli's remaining money. The two stood face-to-face. The purser, who wore an ill-fitting uniform, was the same height as Eli. His thinning hair barely covered his large skull. "That's a nice scarf you have," he continued, as his outstretched arm handed Eli the package. He held his hand in place for a few moments, expecting a small recompense for his act of kindness. Some small token in cash or, if he were lucky, the red scarf. It would make a nice gift for a wife who constantly nagged him. He pictured her face as he arrived home, triumphantly handing over his prize. His house, which was of very modest construction, lay on the Southside of Creighton Street, situated just three blocks from the docks.

Eli tore the package containing his money from the man's hand, and turned, walking directly towards the nearest gangway and his path to anonymity.

"What a bastard, I hope he chokes on that scarf," said the now-disgruntled man thinking of yet another evening with his badgering wife ahead.

Eli vanished into the crowds milling about the docks as the ship prepared to sail. He didn't once take time to look back. Within the hour, the ship would have sailed and all the taverns would be full of the impoverished dockland workforce. Eli, who was hungry and thirsty, decided to fuel up for the journey ahead. Yarmouth was some distance to travel, and a few tentative enquiries may just lead to securing suitable transportation out of Halifax.

Lower Water Street ran parallel to the seafront. Dominated by a row of pale, stone, three-story buildings, the area was constantly busy, and this afforded Eli ample cover to wander along without drawing any undue attention. The large structures housed a variety of businesses as well as a number of domestic residences. Among the first-floor commercial establishments was the less than spacious Red Stag Inn. Many mariners, who cared little about its primitive decoration, frequented the drinking hole. They judged the establishment on the basis that they would be left alone to pour their individual worries into a cheap libation.

Eli stepped into the Red Stag, needing a few moments for his eyes to adjust to the darkness. His nose, similarly, needed a moment to adjust to the smell. A rich cocktail of sweat, beer, onions, and smoke assaulted his senses. The front door opened into a square room that housed four separate seating booths. To the right was a long counter made from a solid-looking piece of dark timber. Behind the worktop stood a short, corpulent, middle-aged woman with a distinctly hairy, pointed chin. Eli was immediately struck by how ugly she was, yet in a strange way, couldn't keep his eyes off her. He slowly approached the bar, noting the four other customers who seemed completely disinterested in him.

"We have rum, ale, or whiskey to drink and chowder to

eat, so what's your poison?" said the sour-faced, unattractive lady, before he had the chance to speak.

"Rude and ugly, a frightful combination," Eli quietly retorted to no-one in particular.

"You'll have to speak up or piss off. I'm going to be busy very shortly, there's a big ship just leaving and they'll be wanting ale," she said, without an ounce of hospitality.

"Ale and a cup of chowder it is then." Eli was left shaking his head at the bar, as the barmaid scuttled off to fetch his soup.

Retreating to a dark recess, he sat at a table so that he had a good view of the front door. It was important that he would not be taken unaware if, by some miracle, Jacob and his strange friend walked in. The clam chowder was surprisingly tasty, and he wondered if he should order another cup. In the booth to his right, a dark-haired man was moaning that he had to travel to the Bay of Fundy and had not had a day off for five weeks. His companion dutifully nodded, although secretly was glad that the man opposite would soon be leaving. Eli listened intently. Perhaps his fate was predetermined after all, meaning that he was, in all probability, untouchable.

Food and drink finished, Eli followed the dark-haired man from the Red Stag. He had tied the red scarf tightly around his head, covering both ears.

"Excuse me, I believe that you are heading for the Bay of Fundy. Would there be any chance that I may accompany you?"

"Get lost before I kick your teeth out."

"I can only give you a few dollars but I will be no trouble and, having experience with horses, will be able to assist you. You could get some rest on the journey."

The dark-haired stranger stopped, taking time to consider Eli's offer. He could certainly do with some sleep, and a little extra cash was indeed an attractive proposition. Having said that, the last thing he needed was constant conversation from anyone – he was only really comfortable in the company of those he knew well or those too inebriated to notice his social awkwardness. Having weighed up the value or otherwise of having a travel companion, he reluctantly agreed to take this stranger with him.

23

The Manifest

"NO-ONE OF THAT NAME IS ON my list. No Eli James here, see for yourself." The large, balding man in the harbourmaster's office pointed to the scruffy piece of paper tethered to his clipboard. "Scott Briggs has another list, mind you."

"Where might I find this Scott Briggs?" enquired Jacob.

"He is on the barge until she sails out past McNab's Island. I reckon he will be back in about an hour, give or take."

Jacob was deflated. He had followed a hunch, putting himself in Eli's shoes, if you will, and now it seemed that he had been wrong. Halifax was an easy place to get lost in if you desired, and the thought that Eli could be anywhere troubled him. A thought jumped into his head. "Do you see many persons travelling alone?"

"Not many, to be honest, mostly family groups. That's not to say that everyone travels accompanied. But I have just two on my list, that's two out of sixty three." He tapped the clipboard and held it up for Jacob to see.

"Right, so if Eli was actually on board he would stand

out, wouldn't he?"

"Perhaps he would, but you must remember, when a ship sails for somewhere like Liverpool there are many people on board. Not only passengers, many just there to say goodbye to people they know. Sometimes it's chaos, and to be frank, it becomes a struggle to ensure that everyone who should get off does so."

Jacob considered the possibility that this was exactly the sort of situation that played into Eli's hands. Confusion and crowds, the perfect place to initiate a deception.

"Maybe if you told me what he looked like, what he wore, it may ring a bell with me. Although I did talk to a lot of people this morning."

"Eli is about this much taller than me and has jet black hair, which appears as if it is constantly wet. He was wearing a navy blue overcoat when I last saw him. And, oh yes, he wore a bright red scarf about his neck. More of an accessory a lady would wear. He may have used the name Cole Haas or Robert Madder. Did you happen to see anyone like that?"

"None of those names rings a bell with me or are on my list. Your description does match someone I spoke to on the upper deck though, just before the ship sailed. Horrible he was, and my wife would have loved that red scarf. Couldn't wait to get off. I watched him all the way to the edge of Water Street."

"Are you sure he got off the ship?"

"Yes, that I am."

"I must confirm that he is not on the passenger list. Is it possible for me to wait for Briggs in here?"

"Sure you can, nothing to me. I have to wait till he returns anyhow."

The hour passed slowly, as it often does when you wait for someone or something.

Scott Briggs loved his work, and carried out every task diligently and with precision. He entered the office in the same manner. His paperwork was all filled out correctly, and his uniform was so neatly pressed one would have assumed that he came directly from the tailor's rather than from the oily barge that had just arrived back into the harbour. His economical use of movement was impressive as he glided past Jacob to take a seat behind the mahogany desk at the back of the office. Briggs moved with a certain grace, at odds with the majority of men that worked in or about the harbour. Finely-framed glasses sat atop a reedy nose, delicately-balanced yet never seemingly at risk from falling to the floor.

"All done," he said, as he slammed shut the top drawer. Without acknowledging Jacob's presence at all, he slowly looked toward his work colleague. "Who do we have here, Jarvis?"

"This young fella is looking for someone who goes by the name of Eli James. He believes he may be on board the ship heading for England."

"Could you please check the list of passengers, Mr Briggs?" enquired Jacob, who was patiently waiting for information.

"That's against company regulations. The list is not for any Tom, Dick, or Harry to look at." Briggs ran his bony fingers through his dark brown hair as he spoke. Then, curiously, ran his thumb across his fingers in a circular motion, at such a rapid rate that it sounded like sandpaper on wood.

"Stop messing with the boy and show him the list, Scott, I need to lock up and get home."

"That's not possible." Scott Briggs said, with a dismissive wave of his hand.

"Please, can you help me?" Jacob said, opening his green eyes as wide as possible to assume the look of a wounded puppy.

Briggs considered the request, taking enough time to enhance the feeling of his authority. "I can only confirm or deny if a name is on the list. You cannot look at it yourself. That is all I offer, no more without the correct legal authority."

"Thank you, sir. The name is Eli James, or it could be Cole Haas, or," Jacob thought for a moment, as Eli would. "Jacob Madder as well, can you check all three? I would be very grateful."

Briggs purposefully unlocked and then pulled open the top drawer to his desk. Wetting his thumb by licking it with his snake-like tongue, he flicked through the pages, mumbling names out loud as he ran an index finger from top to bottom. On the third page he paused. "Eli James, you say?"

"Yes, that's right." said Jacob, who could not hide his disappointment that Eli may well have got on board.

"I can confirm that Eli James is on my list. So, if that's all, I must ask you to leave, young man."

"I know what I saw, and what I saw was a fella wearing a red scarf leave the harbour and heading up Water Street," said the fat, balding man, who quite obviously detested the fishiness of his colleague. "List or no list, the lad you describe never sailed."

"Don't be stupid, Jackson. The manifest does not lie, and why would anyone pay a not-so-insignificant sum of money just to leave the boat before it set sail? It would be madness, like throwing cash into the sea. Is this Eli James made of money? Anyway, enough questions, we must lock up the office now. Have you both not homes to go to?"

Jacob was crushed, fearing that Eli had got away after all. Head bowed, he slowly left the harbour master's office, stepping out into a bitter wind that had arrived unannounced. As is often the case in the Maritimes, the weather had turned at the drop of a hat. Jacob looked out to sea, to where great dark clouds hung over the water like a menacing messenger about to unleash a storm. From where he stood, he could hear Scott Briggs turning the key to lock the office door. It wasn't the thin man's fault that Eli had gone, yet Jacob didn't like his manner at all. Maybe Jacob's disappointment was allowing him to be less than generous in his feelings for a man he barely knew?

"Where are you heading for?" Jarvis enquired, with a degree of warmth in his gravelly voice. "That storm is going to hit tonight, so you best get to where you're going. I wouldn't recommend being out on the harbour when she arrives."

"I am going back to St. Paul's and then, to be honest, I have no clue where I might go."

"Listen, I am serious when I say I saw that boy leave the boat. Briggs is efficient, yes, but…" He hesitated, as if he were about to tell this stranger an important secret. "Don't tell anyone I said this. You go digging up a barrel of worms and my name gets bandied about in the wrong circles, I will definitely lose my job. There are some itching to get rid of me so I can't give 'em any excuse. You understand what I'm saying, Jacob Madder?"

"I promise I will not say anything to anyone, Jarvis."

"You saw what Briggs is like. Thinks he does everything well, he does. So his list is always perfect, right? Wrong. I know for a fact that there have been ships sailed from Halifax with names of people who weren't on board. One time, about six months ago I think, a whole family – five of 'em – had their names on the list to sail to England on a big steamer. I forget the name of the boat, but then two days after she sailed they walk into the harbour master's office, wanting to speak to Briggs about their mother, who had forgotten something or other. Papers, I think, for when she arrived in Liverpool. Briggs was busy with the ink that day, I tell you. Point is, Jacob, these lists are not as conclusive as they lead you to believe. Perhaps this Eli wanted to make people think he was headed out to sea? Maybe the guy I saw head off down Water Street was this Eli? I might be wrong, but if I was in your shoes, I would keep my mind open to the possibility that he is still in Nova Scotia."

"Thank you, Jarvis. I appreciate you telling me this. I am convinced he will not be on that boat."

"No problem, but as I said, you made a promise to me that you won't go to the ship's office and say anything. I would have to deny we had this conversation."

"I will be leaving Halifax for sure, Jarvis, so don't worry. I will not tell a soul what you have said."

"Ok, well, be careful, young man, and get to the church on Barrington before this storm hits. Oh, and, by the way, my name is William. Bill, to my friends."

"Goodbye, Bill, and thanks again." Jacob left for Barrington Street with a new spring in his step. Sorrow and terror over lost friends were forgotten, at least for the time being. He was determined to stay hot on the trail and find Eli before he could hurt another girl.

"Thomsen, Thomsen, where are you?" Jacob's voice echoed about the empty church. "I have news of Eli." The door slammed shut behind him as he rushed forward towards the pulpit.

Rain hammered onto the roof of St. Paul's, the shingles batting back the torrent in a constant drumroll. Inside, Father Laybolt was labouring due to the knife wound as he prepared a hot drink. Thomsen was sitting quietly in the corner, patiently waiting for some sustenance. Father Laybolt was not known for his silence, but it seemed appropriate to him to meekly go about his task. Thomsen, of course, was naturally comfortable not talking at all. The singing kettle, having reached boiling point, broke the silence with a shrill whistle.

Cup of steaming tea in hand, Thomsen could hear words, faintly at first, as if they were originating from someone locked inside a box. As Jacob approached the tiny kitchen situated just behind the two rooms designated for confessionals, he couldn't contain his excitement. Yet the sanctity of the building caused him to speak in a lower register, almost whispering, "Thomsen I have news. We must head out of Halifax. Where are you?"

Returning the cup to the oak table in front of him, Thomsen glanced up at Father Laybolt, who had also heard Jacob arrive and was already shuffling towards the door.

"I'm glad you're back in one piece, Jacob, I was truly worried that you would have confronted that monster alone." Father Laybolt held his arms out wide to receive Jacob as he spoke. Thomsen stood behind the cleric, patiently awaiting his turn to greet his friend.

"He didn't get on the boat, Thomsen. I believe I know where he is heading, but we must first return to Oak Island. I need to see if Eve is ok. I fear for her and hope with all my heart she is still alive."

"Best get my coat then," said Thomsen.

"Jacob, wait, I have something for you before you leave,"

said Father Laybolt, as he pressed a small envelope into Jacob's hand. "You will need this money to pay for your journey. I cannot think of a better use for it."

"I will pay you back, father. You can count on it."

24

Yarmouth

BRADLEY WILSON WAS AN OLD MAN. A lonely man, who was unaccustomed, in recent times, to nice things coming his way. He had lived in the same house in Yarmouth his whole life. He was born in the small bedroom at the top of the stairs, married Margaret in the front drawing room, conceived each one of their four children in just two rooms – the aforementioned main bedroom and the floor of the modest service kitchen – and he would most surely die in his bed, here at number 225 Main Street.

The house had, in its day, been the grand home of a successful sea captain. The captain had – despite an abundance of local wood being readily available – had wood shipped all the way from England for construction of his home. The house was his final attempt to keep his wayward daughter, Anne, happy. Alas, the girl was tempted by a handsome French sailor and had disappeared, leaving her father broken-hearted. The advent of the steamships had hastened the end of the golden age of the sail, and the captain quickly fell upon hard times. He was forced to sell the newly-built house to Wilson's father in 1765.

Bradley, or Bladders to Yarmouthians, was widowed in 1844. His three children, who had all left Yarmouth, seldom visited. The old man rattled around the house, which had rooms that had not been used for years. Despite several generous offers, he refused to sell the house and was determined to end his days as he began them; in the bedroom at the top of the stairs. Bladders was a kind man, and even when he was under the influence, which was quite frankly most of his waking hours, hence the name, he often greeted strangers enthusiastically.

So it was that, as the nephew he had never known arrived at the red front door of the Wilson house, he was greeted as a long-lost child.

"Come in, come in. Take a seat in front of the fire and I'll fetch us a dram." Bladders was so excited to have company that it mattered little that he didn't know Eli by sight.

It was a strange twist of fate that Eli had been led to this particular residence. There were close to fifty other doors he could have tried before number 225, yet as he approached the door to this house, he knew that his uncle lived here. He was relieved that, after yet another arduous journey of looking over his shoulder and being wary of everyone he met, he would have a roof over his head for the first time in five days.

"Oh, thank you, sir," said a weary Eli as he crossed the slate threshold leading through to a most cluttered reception room. Bladders Wilson never threw away anything. The small house was filled with strange and wonderful objects collected from a lifetime living so close to the ocean. There were copper kettles and lanterns, and foreign-looking objects everywhere.

Wilson was rushing from room to room on the ground floor; he was keen to make a favourable impression on his unexpected visitor. His flushed cheeks seemed redder than usual as he returned with two large glasses of rum. Eli downed the alcohol at once, sending him into a coughing spree.

"Oh dear, oh dear, perhaps I should have brought some water for you?"

"Mr Wilson. You don't know who I am, do you?"

"Yes, of course I do, you're Elisabeth's boy, aren't you? I would recognise those eyes anywhere."

Eli was astounded that this apparent chump was perhaps sharper than he had first thought.

"Have you been told of your father's brother?" Wilson asked. "You know, he also tends a light. In Chatham, on the cape. By all accounts, it's a beautiful place."

"No, I know of no such relative." Eli was suddenly intrigued to learn that the family tree had branches he knew nothing of.

"Yes, Robert's brother holds a secret. A doozy of one, I can tell you."

"What secret?"

"This family is full of secrets, lad. Did you know you have a half-sister?"

"I have a sister?" Eli was astounded by this latest

revelation. "You must tell me, is she still in Nova Scotia?"

"Oh, yes she is, a bit of a sad tale. They all think I never listen, but I'll tell you, lad, people who visit me rarely stop talking. They think I won't remember due to the drink, you know, but I never forget a thing. Memory like that elephant over there I have." He laughed as he pointed to a small, intricately-carved elephant on the shelf above the fireplace. "I'm not so sure I should tell you things that concern your father though. I never liked him, weasel of a man, no match for a girl filled with Wilson blood. Then again, I suppose I won't be seeing him anytime soon, so maybe you should know a thing or two about your sister?"

"Go on, old man." Eli was growing impatient with Bradley and his unpleasant voice.

"Ok, Ok. Your pa was unhappy with home life and found himself in the woods with a beautiful woman. Let me think, near Chester way. Oak Island, that's it! Well he was partial to a bit of fucking, your father. Problem is, the woman fell pregnant and her husband didn't care for young'uns. So she forced him, against his wishes, to take care of the girl until she was older. Then he talked his wife into buggering off – and they left the girl to fend for herself, never told your father. Trouble was, the husband came to Yarmouth and, well, I think he'd bottled up his tale for too long and I happened to be the drunk at the end of the bar who he told!"

Eli fell back in his chair, the shock of what the old man had said slowly sinking in.

"Surely, it's not that bad, boy? It would be a good thing to reacquaint yourself with your kin, and going from what I heard, she's done pretty well for herself."

Eli was ashen-faced as the truth of what he had done dawned on him. Not realising that his own words had revealed something terrible, Bradley leaned in, thinking that the real family secret would lighten the boy's mood.

"Now, let me whisper that even bigger secret to you, lad, about the money they stole from me!"

Wilson cupped his hands round his mouth as he whispered the family secret to his nephew.

Without a word, Eli got up and walked out of the house. The red front door slammed behind him as he headed south, up Main Street, turning into Argyle Street, then quickly onto Water Street and to the main dock area. He hoped that the ferry heading for Maine would be running. The route had only just been established and, due to a number of teething problems, was less than reliable. In subsequent years, following some horrific crossings, the ferry only ran for five months per year. It was fortunate that, on this particular day, the captain of the ferry was a man full of bravado. "No ice or storm will stop me!" he claimed.

Eli stood on the deck as the ferry left Yarmouth, taking one last, lingering look at the Canadian coastline he left behind. He didn't realise, however, that this would be the last time he would ever see Canada. It was too cold to be outside, so he retreated to the main cabin, whereupon he observed the small group of his fellow passengers huddled around the galley. Finding a place on a wooden seat not too far away from the others, his mind drifted towards arriving in America.

25

The Isner Girls

THE ENGINES DEEP IN THE BOWELS of the boat responded sluggishly to the request of the fearless captain, causing the ferry to lurch to the left in an unstable manner. Without hesitation, he pushed harder on the throttle, whilst aiming the boat into the narrow opening out of Yarmouth harbour. Beyond was open water, the surface of which was already whipping up violently, as the winds grew stronger.

From the row of circular windows that ran the full length of the main cabin area, the small number of horrified passengers looked out. The stone embankment that ran along each side of the harbour seemed to move towards them, tormenting and threatening like a giant, gloved hand, unwilling to let them leave.

"This is madness, we are going to drown," shouted a very pale-looking man, who was quite clearly on the cusp of seasickness. "I want to get off, where's the captain?" He ran towards the bow of the ferry. Before reaching the door to outside, and ultimately, the pilothouse, he doubled up, depositing the contents of his stomach onto the floor in one ferocious surge. Assuming the foetal position, he lay on the ground next to his vomit and commenced rocking from side to side. Not one of the passengers went over to assist the poor man. Eli rolled his eyes and turned away to look again at the closing in of the harbour walls. He wasn't afraid and smiled as he saw the sheer horror on the faces of the others.

"What are you laughing about, shithead?"

Eli had gained the attention of a large, fearsome Canadian who sat opposite. He had a square jaw and dark, deep-set brown eyes. His nose was crooked like that of a professional boxer with a very poor record of winning. His shoulders must have measured three feet wide, and an unusually narrow waist made his body appear to belong to two entirely separate men. Eli guessed, correctly, that his profession was based in lumber. The man's nose had most probably been broken by some wayward piece of timber hitting him squarely in the face. Eli noticed that the lumberman's hands gripped the wooden seat so tightly that his knuckles – seemingly devoid of any blood – were white.

"No offence intended, mister. I just get a bit kiddy when faced with fear." Eli said, trying to be heard above the resonating sound of the steam engine.

"Ok, fella, but just think about the others, especially those two over there." He pointed to two girls, obviously sisters, who were hugging each other for dear life. Eli thought it strange that he hadn't noticed the girls before now. As he studied them he inadvertently protruded his tongue between his teeth and licked his lips.

Mary-Beth and Susan Isner heralded from Portland, Maine. They had spent the last three months in Yarmouth at the behest of their grandmother, Irene Isner. Old Maid Isner, a widow, was a woman you could never say no to. She had instructed her son Ernst – the girls' father – to pack his two daughters off to spend the summer with her, where they were to be educated in the deportment required to be a lady.

"Standards are slipping with the younger girls today. I will not let that happen to an Isner girl, not as long as I live and breathe," the old woman had told her put-upon son. Being an Isner girl meant commitment to following in the footsteps of a long line of women who knew their place in the world. Irene was concerned that the younger generation would grow to become independent and too strong-willed for any future husband. Her role was to remind the two sixteen-year-olds of what was expected of them by any suitable beau.

Consequently, the two girls had spent the sixteenth summer of their lives being schooled on how to become old-fashioned. They were desperate to return to Maine and as such were elated when old Ms Isner had taken a sudden turn for the worse. They were instructed to go home via the Yarmouth ferry, rather than travel over land to Halifax then on to a long, arduous rail journey through New Brunswick.

As the two girls sat, shaking with fear, they simultaneously became racked with guilt. Firstly, about the old matriarch they had been so desperate to get away from, and secondly about badgering Miss Frost – their grandmother's live-in nurse – to book them on the first available ferry. Taking into account their youthfulness and hitherto lack of experience, they were still intelligent enough to assume correctly that any future ferry crossings could, and probably would, have fallen victim to even worse weather. Nevertheless, they now considered the teachings of Irene Isner to be a considerably more suitable prospect than possible death by drowning.

The ferry tilted precariously again, causing the door to the passenger area to spring open. A howling sound filled the cabin as the Canadian lumberjack leapt from his seat to try and close the door. Sea spray covered his angular face as he applied his large hands to the insubstantial wooden door. The Canadian was amazed by the effort needed to complete the task. One of the crew suddenly appeared in the doorway. In his hand was a length of thick rope, which he quickly lashed around the handle of the door.

"Should we be thinking of turning back to Yarmouth?" shouted the Canadian.

"You try and tell the captain, we think he has lost his mind," replied the young sailor. Working together, they managed to close the door and tie the rope in such a fashion that the door would not open again so easily. It didn't cross anyone's mind that if the ferry sank they would most certainly be trapped inside.

Eli heard the two girls squeal as they were thrown against the sidewall of the cabin, their small faces pressed against the thick glass of the window, looking very much like startled animals caught in gaslight. Through the window, they were now looking directly down into the inky, raging water. Fear was etched on their youthful faces. Quick as a flash, Eli moved to the seat beside them, extending his arm around the slender shoulders of Mary-Beth.

"Hold onto me and link your arms together. The boat will right itself shortly, and once we get out of the bay it should get easier," Eli said, with as much sincerity as he could muster. His slick black hair glistened in the unusual light of the cabin.

"Oh, thank you, we are very grateful. Do you think they will turn back for Yarmouth?" said the older sister.

"Come on, there really is only a slim chance that the ship will sink. Just think of this as a great adventure," replied Eli.

"What is your name? We would like to know who it is that has assisted us."

"It is my pleasure to help two such lovely girls. I promise you, we will get through this. My name is Jacob, Jacob Madder. I am very pleased to make your acquaintance."

Susan Isner unexpectedly reached over and clasped her arms around Eli's waist. The hug lasted for a few minutes. Eli drew in deep breaths of the delicate soapy fragrance about her neck and hair. This was a most unexpected gratuity. Eli once again felt the stirrings, a sensation he was familiar with, and one that he liked.

Finally, the ferry was out in open water, and the captain was skilled enough to steady the boat to a less precarious pitching. Inside, the passengers remained in a state of unease that would probably last until they reached Portland. The two Isner girls were sat together; Mary-Beth looked particularly dishevelled, which was unpleasant for a self-conscious teenager. She was keen to find a rest-room where she could tidy herself up. Susan was similarly desperate to go to the toilet; she was uncomfortably damp from sweating while the ferry had been trying to navigate out of the harbour.

Eli had now returned to his own seat, directly opposite the two girls. He was staring at Susan. There was a strange familiarity about her that he couldn't quite put his finger on. He now had the time to study her closely, without worrying about the ferry capsizing. She was very pretty.

The crossing became – compared to the drama at the start of the voyage – relatively uneventful. The swell was at over eight feet high, but to a boat the size of the Yarmouth ferry, this presented no problem. The captain was still not able to relax; he knew these skies, and directly before the ship lay some very menacing clouds.

Experience told him to expect the worst yet he hoped that they would be able to get to the safety of Maine before the storm hit. Unaware of what lay ahead, the passengers could finally relax. Indeed, they had returned to idle chatter and reflecting on whether the captain was foolhardy or an excellent mariner. After a further hour, the passengers had fallen silent. Some were reading, whilst others tried to sleep. Upon instruction from his captain, the youngest crewmember was carefully making his way through the cabin, offering sweet tea and oat biscuits. The last thing the captain needed when they finally reached port was complaints concerning his gung-ho approach to sailing.

The last of the daylight leaked through a crack in the cloud cover, as the ferry slowly made headway towards Maine. The threatening veil ahead held an unwelcome guest, heralded by a loud rumble. The first flash of light surprised crew and passengers alike, who ran for cover inside the main cabin. The captain was holding the wheel as tightly as he could manage, whilst barking out orders to a crew mainly made up of young sailors who were as frightened as the passengers.

Eli was making his way along one of the corridors below deck. Like a drunk, he used both walls to gradually push towards the compartments designated for use by crewmembers only. He wanted to find a suitable place to deal with the younger of the Isner girls.

The Isner girls were still sat very close to the Canadian lumberjack on the upper deck, and seasickness had made all three feel queasy. Susan was holding up slightly better than her sister and was dispatched, before the storm intensified, to find some drinking water below deck. Having navigated the narrow iron stairs towards the rear of the cabin, descending as carefully as she could, she found herself at the end of an oppressive corridor. Heat generated from the thrusting of the engine hung in the air, making it hard to breathe. The storm outside was intensifying, and the ferry returned to the violent pitching they had endured in Yarmouth Harbour.

There was a crack as the ferry shifted again; Susan stiffened as she stared into the dense murk, struggling to focus in the gloom. Seawater laced with rust ran over her dainty white shoes as the boat swayed, and she worried that the expensive footwear would be ruined. She leaned against the bolted wall and told herself not to panic; just find the galley and return above deck as soon as possible.

"Is this what you're looking for?"

She had neither seen nor heard Eli approach. He now stood, holding a flask in his outstretched hand.

"Oh, it's you, thank goodness! I was worried I wouldn't find my way around down here. It's horrible below deck, can we go back together?"

Eli held out his other hand, beckoning her to take hold. As her fingers met his, he grabbed her wrists and dropped the flask, which rolled from side to side in time with the movement of the ferry. He dragged her quickly into the nearest room and slammed shut the metal door behind them.

Susan Isner listened to her own terrified breathing as she blinked in the darkness. She sat on the cold metal floor in a corner of the small crew room, deep inside the ferry. The beautifully-laced dress, which had been a Christmas gift from her father, was ripped open at the neck and now hung loose around her midriff. Mottled red marks were prevalent around her neck and bosom, where blood had been drawn to the surface by the pressure of his grip. Three six-inch scratches ran from just below her left ear to the hollow above her sternum.

The ferry pitched violently to one side, causing a metal cup to roll noisily across the mess table. There was a rumble of thunder, followed by another lightning bolt that shone a temporary white light upon Eli's face. He wore a chilling smile. As quickly as it came, the light was gone, and the room once again was thrown into darkness. Susan blinked rapidly, trying to adjust to the dark. The only things visible were the drops of sea spray slowly running down the glass of the small porthole, mirroring the tears that ran down her cheeks.

Such was the demand for the crew to be fully engaged during the storm that it was highly unlikely that any of them would turn up to save her. Eli knew this would be a place where they would not be disturbed. He had time to experiment.

"Is it not nice when the things you least expect, happen? I love the unexpected nature of things. Who would have thought that the maelstrom of this voyage could present to me – well, you?" he asked her.

As he moved towards her for a second time, he vacillated over whether or not to fill her mouth with something to stop the anticipated screaming. But for now, she was not screaming, just frozen in fear. This was not like Nancy, so he continued.

His full weight felt heavy on her small chest, as his hands

moved up between her legs. Her skin was soft and warm, which excited him. She didn't blink; her eyes stayed fully open in a bewildered stare. She did not resist, which was unexpected. He stopped, looking directly at her face, recoiling in disbelief; Susan Isner wore the face of Nancy Haas. Shaking his head to clear his mind he looked again, this time relieved to see that it was only that Susan looked so similar to Nancy. Perhaps he wasn't being haunted after all, and it was only his imagination that raised the similarity between the faces of two completely different girls.

The door to the crew room flew open; the distinctive blue light radiating from the small kerosene lamp that hung on the wall outside flooded the room. Eli retreated quickly into the shadows, as Mary-Beth Isner raced towards the stricken Susan, lying against the far wall. Mary-Beth instantly removed her coat to cover her half-naked sister. A movement from behind her caught her eye and she turned, just in time to see a shadowy figure go out into the corridor. Jumping up, she quickly followed the figure into the corridor, but he was gone. Deciding that her sister's needs were of greater importance and should warrant her attention, she returned to comfort Susan.

Having delivered her sister to safety, Mary-Beth decided to return to the passenger cabin to collect their belongings. She would then ask the captain if they could both stay in the pilothouse until they reached Portland. There were only fifteen feet between the passenger cabin and the entrance to where the captain was stationed, even though her arms were laden with luggage, she felt capable of navigating the distance safely. Trying to balance on the wet decking boards was tricky, and she found herself using both the small rail that ran the full length of the ferry and the cabin wall for stability. Waiting for the pitch, she rested momentarily, pressed against the rail, hoping that as soon as the boat moved back to the left she would use this momentum to arrive at the door of the pilothouse. It was this hesitation that cost her dearly.

Eli saw his opportunity and, quick as a flash, scanned the area to see if anyone else was present. When he was sure that they were alone, he rushed behind her and pushed. It didn't take a great deal of effort to shove her over; she didn't weigh a great deal and he had timed it perfectly in unison with the pitching of the ferry. Only a modicum of effort was required to propel her over the low rail. Mary-Beth flew head-first into the freezing water. Within six minutes, she had stopped breathing, within ten, her brain had suffered severe neurological damage. The last image she held was of the ferry disappearing into the distance and of Eli leaning against the rail, slowly waving at her. Swallowed by the water, she never resurfaced. Her body would never be found.

"Help! She's gone overboard. Lost her balance, I tried to save her but it was just too late," Eli said as he ran through the door to the pilothouse. Several members of the young crew were frantically rushing about as the captain tried to plot a safe course through the storm.

"What's that you say?" enquired a small man in the distinctive uniform of the Yarmouth Ferry Company.

"Girl overboard, girl overboard!" Eli shouted.

The captain instantly signalled for the engine to be turned off and held out his hand to beckon Eli towards him. "What did you say, son?"

"There's a girl gone over the rail on the starboard side, sir. Just a few minutes ago, I couldn't reach her. She went under the water and I didn't see her come back up."

Susan Isner stood to the rear of the small box that housed the ship's wheel, worry etched across her pallid, bruised face. She would not say a word for many weeks It would be said that her voice was lost when her sister drowned.

Now that the captain has commenced full emergency procedures, the whole crew were fully occupied by the measures set out by the Ferry Company. Men were running up and down the main deck looking out into the dark water for any sign of Mary Beth. The captain wrestled with the ship's wheel trying to turn the ferry around. Eli, meanwhile, found himself in the far corner of the pilothouse with Susan, who was shaking like a leaf stood at his side. He leaned over, as she recoiled in horror, fearing a repeat of what had happened below deck.

"You say one word of what you think I did to you, and I will find you, and this time, it will be much worse." As he spoke, he held the small knife – the one he had kept from his time with his half-sister – against her throat. "Sharp, isn't it? I will come to you in your sleep and run this blade deep into you. Stay silent and, as you are so pretty, I will allow you to live."

The ferry was only one hour from Portland. Despite the tragedy, the captain made the brave decision to continue onward. This was a better proposition than turning round, as his crew was exhausted and the storm still raged behind them. He would return to Yarmouth as soon as the weather allowed, and an investigation could commence. As far as he was concerned, the drowning of Mary-Beth Isner was a tragic accident, one with no suspicious circumstances. Besides, it was her mistake to be in an area where passengers were forbidden. Only Susan knew that the death of her sister was no accident, and she was too afraid to speak up.

As Eli's thoughts returned to the possibility that there may be a stash of money beneath the lighthouse in Chatham, he reflected for a short time about Jacob. He missed having a friend. A friend he could always control. And now, as he contemplated his new life as William Jacobson, he wondered if he would ever be able to call anyone a friend again.

Only in Chatham would he discover if there was any substance to what the old man had said. That must be his focus, he decided, as he looked into his hand at the final dollar of his mother's money. To start a new life in a new country would need a certain level of funding, and 'Jacobson' possessed few of the qualities that were needed to secure honest paid work.

26

The Truth is Out

JACOB, WITH A MUCH-HEGHTENED LEVEL of trepidation, pushed open the wooden door to Eve's modest home. The rusting hinge grated as he applied his shoulder to the task of fully opening the door. It was the smell that hit him first. His hope that she was still alive all but vanished in that single moment. Then he heard the flies. It was so dark inside that his first task had to be to open the heavy wooden shutters that covered all the windows. He suddenly wished that he had not asked Thomsen to remain at the inn in Chester, yet he knew he must do this alone.

As the first strands of light illuminated the main living area, he noticed the large form of Eve's beloved dog slumped against the doorway to the rear of the cabin. Beside Skipper's body was a pool of something like congealed treacle, that had oozed from a gaping wound just below the dog's shoulders. Jacob recoiled, holding his hand firmly over his mouth. As he crept forward, Skipper's body suddenly jolted. Jacob fell to his knees, reaching out with an innocent hope that it was not too late to help this poor animal. As his hand reached Skipper's body, a huge rat sprang out of the crudely torn injury. The rodent was covered in a slick viscid gloop. It squealed and ran into the dark recess behind the old stove. Jacob gagged, spitting forth foamy, bile-filled saliva.

"Poor Skipper." He whispered to himself. He had grown fond of the dog in the few days he had spent in the woods. The bond between Eve and her pet represented loyalty and trust. His green eyes filled with tears as he edged away from the corpse of the dog, carefully stepping over him as he reached for the metal handle of the door.

Darkness can shroud a multitude of sins, yet as he pushed open the door to Eve's bedroom, Jacob already knew what he would find. Her naked body was placed upright on the bed, visible as the shaft of light illuminated the awful scene. Jacob expelled a harrowing moan as he absorbed what lay in front of him. He tried to breathe in, deep and slow, in order to control his pulse, which had begun to race. An impulse to flee flooded his mind, yet something told him to take in as many details as he could. There was something all-too familiar before him.

Fighting back the tears, he removed the wooden shutter from the window beside her bed. His mouth filled with a bitter taste as he tried to control the urge to vomit. In his eyes, she was still beautiful. He felt embarrassed as he looked at her private parts. It was wrong to have any thoughts other than sorrow at this point. Then the anger commenced. He noticed that her face was contorted, and upon closer inspection, it was evident that there was something stuffed into her mouth.

Eve's body had slowly begun to break down. Given the cold temperature inside – without the fire, which had long gone out – it would take much longer for her to decompose. The swelling of her torso had only just started to alter her form. Save for her contorted mouth, she looked asleep. He looked for something to cover her with. It would be some time before others would discover her, and he wanted to protect her innocence. The thought of someone else seeing her in this state of undress upset Jacob, and, using a spare bed quilt, he covered her up to the neck. He failed to notice the beautiful blue-and-yellow pattern of strange and beautiful fish that had been painstakingly crafted by one of the fishermen's wives and given to Eve as a Christmas present.

He felt that he should stay with her for a longer time, but that was nonsensical. She was never going to wake and give him one of her wonderful smiles. Besides, the quicker he got back to the inn at Chester where Thomsen waited, the quicker he could set off in pursuit of Eli.

"Why would he be in Yarmouth, anyway?" Thomsen had asked, curiously. "Not many go there out of choice. A good place to hide, I grant you. It's got a lot of rough edges, has Yarmouth, and too many old mariners partial to drink and brawling."

"He will go south, Thomsen, for two reasons. Firstly, he has kin who can help him. His mother told me of an estranged, wealthy man that they seldom had dealings with. Secondly, when we were younger he always talked of going to Boston, it was a dream of his. As you say, there are many individuals who choose to live somewhere where people don't ask too many questions. My father told me of his time in Yarmouth and I have a hunch that it would be the perfect place to get over the border to America."

"Fair point, you may well be right. There's only one way to find out, isn't there?"

Jacob and Thomsen secured passage to Yarmouth. Ben Johnson, an illiterate itinerant, travelled between Chester and Yarmouth only twice per year, conveying a variety of goods. In fact, for a modest recompense, he would take anything and everything. Once he had even transported a man from Truro to Digby who was Arabian by birth and spoke neither English nor French. It had been a quiet journey and had been noted for his passenger getting into a frightful argument after slaughtering a domestic goat in Annapolis.

They found Johnson in the bar of the Ship's Inn in Chester. Exactly where the landlord said he would be. He was hard to miss as he wobbled on a rickety stool at the far end of the room.

Johnson was a man firmly set in his ways. Completely bald and boggle-eyed, he had carried people's chattels for many years to various parts of the province. His gnarled hands, seemingly stuck in the position they adopted whilst gripping the reins, made him look as though he was about to pounce at any given moment. He had never married and, as far as anyone could tell, had no kin whatsoever. It would be a long journey, given that Ben Johnson travelled at his own pace, and no cock-a-hoop story of chasing someone would change that.

"Five dollars each, that's the cost, no return, no haggling. My rules and my time, take it or leave it, you decide. I leave at first light so if you are late, I be gone." Johnson didn't look at them once as he spoke. He knew they had no other option, so held out his curled-up hand, waiting for the ten dollars to be placed there.

There was only a slim hope that they would find Eli, but they had to try. For Nancy and for Eve, he must be caught. It was a hunch, but one that Jacob felt compelled to follow. The constable in Halifax had steadfastly refused to believe that Eli had not boarded the 'City of Boston'. The ship was now confirmed as overdue, and the general consensus was that she had gone down somewhere far out to sea.

"Eli James's name is on the list and he has perished, so in our eyes, has met a suitable end. We shall not be investigating the matter further and suggest that you go back to Sable and tell them what has happened." The words of the officer were still clear in Jacob's mind. All the parts fitted into a neat parcel, no further inquiries, Eli James was deceased – case closed.

"I know he lives, Thomsen, and we must prove it. I will understand if you want no further part in this."

"Listen, Jacob, It's been a while since I have been to Yarmouth. There are a few people I need to catch up with and one man in particular, if the opportunity presents itself, that it would be beneficial for me to see," he lied, there was no man he needed to see and both men knew full well that they would be travelling to Yarmouth together.

Even though it was doubtful that Eli would be easily found, Thomsen was not going to take any chances and let Jacob face a potential threat alone. Not after what had happened in the nave at St. Paul's.

It took four arduous days of travel to arrive in Yarmouth. Ben Johnson was true to his word, and they arrived late on a Wednesday evening. Jacob had told Thomsen that Lisbeth James had mentioned an old eccentric relative who lived in Yarmouth. He even recalled the description of the grand house in which he lived. This was the only information they had to go on. Jacob had asked Johnson if he knew of such a house, to which the traveller had blown a raspberry and said nothing. It was too late to start looking tonight, and they needed to recover from the bone-shaking journey in the back of Johnson's cart.

"Tomorrow, at first light, we will find the house, Thomsen. I can feel him, he has been here, I am sure of it."

It was a chilly morning in Yarmouth as Jacob walked towards another front door and, with low expectations, rattled the knocker. In the two hours since dawn, they had knocked on door after door, usually greeted with curse words or, in one instance, by a bucket of water. Spirits were as damp as the water had been.

Bradley Wilson was more excited than ever. "Another

visitor! My, oh my, this is turning out to be a good week," he said, as he rushed to open the door.

27

Another Bird of Passage

THE NORTH END WAS AS BUSY as it always was. Hustle and bustle presided along each of the four blocks that made up the district called home by many Italian immigrants. They were called "birds of passage" as they all intended to leave once they had made enough money. Unlike the early Jewish settlers to the area, they struggled to make the transition to the American way.

Eli James, now travelling as William Jacobson, had caught the dawn train from Portland, Maine and watched the city wake as he walked from North Station, eastwards, along Boylston Street. Carts loaded with ice were pushed along by young boys, heading for the markets to procure shellfish for the many restaurants of the area. The clattering wooden wheels made such a distinct and recognisable sound that none of the locals turned their heads as the carts rattled by.

It seemed that everyone was in a hurry. The streets were busy with people moving this way and that, afraid that if they were to stop they would return to the lunacy of living. The Irish hated the illiterate Italians, who had to rely on paesani – people from the same Italian villages as them –

to survive. Ironically, a significant proportion of the Irish were similarly unable to read and write. The Italians were wary of being out at night, especially near the waterfront, which was controlled by Irish gangs. It was dangerous for them to try and pass through Irish territory, which could lead to severe consequences.

Although both Irish and Italians were Catholics, the latter formed separate churches. This only further estranged such segregated groups from both the Irish and the Jewish residents, who were suspicious of everyone. When Sicilian fishermen – who often arrived in port during the second week in August – honoured the Madonna at the annual festival, there was an uneasy truce, often only upheld by payment or gifts to powerful Irish gang members. If no premium had been presented, violence and death would have most certainly ensued.

The North End was Boston's "classic land of poverty." Vibrant and tense, it was an exciting place to be. It was also the perfect place for Eli to hide, to disappear into a sea of impoverished immigrants.

Even though his ultimate destination was the lighthouse in Chatham, he gave serious thought to remaining in Boston; he liked the energy of city life. Having only previously known life in a Canadian backwater, he quickly grew intoxicated by being among so many different types of people. This enthusiasm quickly evaporated when he came across Seamus Kelley and his two brothers in an alley behind Hanover Street.

"Siete ok giovane?" Eli did not understand the old man, who was gesticulating at him as he emerged, bloodied and bruised, from behind Hanover Street. He stumbled on the old grey cobbles, using an outstretched arm to cushion his fall. Blood ran from several cuts to his face, and his nose was most certainly broken. Seamus had very hard hands.

The Kelley brothers were well known for bullying anyone unfortunate enough to make their acquaintance. Seamus – the oldest and therefore the self-appointed leader – was a bruiser of a man. His close-cropped red hair sat atop a blotchy, freckled face. He spoke with a strange lisp, and his mouth lacked a number of teeth after a career of brawling for money. Look at him the wrong way and the consequences were dire, as Eli soon found out.

As he lay on those cold cobbles, Eli, now known as William, decided that the sooner he travelled to Chatham and the lighthouse, the better. With his eyes closed, he pushed the pain aside and thought only of the hoard of metal boxes stored underneath the lighthouse. The money would help, and he would not allow the keeper – his uncle – to get in the way, whatever the cost.

"Stai bene?" The old man, who was wearing a heavy woollen suit with a large red flower in the lapel, reached down to touch Eli as he spoke. "You good?" he enquired again, his accent heavily laced by his Venetian heritage.

Eli James was to be a real bird of passage and headed for the station, where he would leave Boston and the North End in particular.

The train pulled into the station through a plume of pale smoke. It was one of the new trains commissioned by JP Morgan for the recently completed route; dark metal, shiny, and loud. Eli was staggered by the cost quoted by the dull ticket clerk for travelling in the Pullman or private cars. He quickly, without the exchange of many words, purchased a one-way ticket to Chatham – a stop on the Hyannis line. As he wandered along the platform, it was a source of irritation that the first-class cars were so splendidly empty. He would have enjoyed the solitude. However, he had reached the last of his money, so his ticket was for the second-class car towards the rear of the train. Climbing aboard, he took the last available seat next to a rather large man, who wore dark blue overalls. The man was splayed across both seats, and was snoring loudly. Eli squeezed himself in and prayed that the journey would feel quicker than it actually was.

In the seat directly opposite was a young, dark-haired woman. She had flaccid, oversized hands that ill-matched a disproportionately tiny body. Her long, oval face seemed at odds with her small frame. Her lips were full and entirely too grown-up for her face, which was still the face of a child. Eli assumed her age to be fourteen or fifteen and wondered why she was travelling alone. Perhaps he would strike up a conversation with her later. He would assume his fake aura of empathy and concern with ease. For now, he was too worked up to switch on a charm offensive. She was his type though, and he certainly held an interest in following her. Her petite breasts heaved, as she suddenly felt uncomfortable on a train predominantly full of men.

The fifteen-minute time allocation for a 'limited express' at the Fred Harvey restaurant elapsed, and the train slowly pulled away from Boston. All second-class passengers had only this brief stop to eat and use the bathroom. If you missed the opportunity by not forwarding an order ahead of time, you relied on the young men who charged from car to car carrying a small array of goods for sustenance.

The blond-haired news butcher shouted loudly as he made his way along the centre of the car in which Eli sat. The noise woke the man sleeping in the seat alongside him. A heated argument ensued between the man and the news butcher, that was only settled when the latter handed over a newspaper and some tobacco free of charge. Eli longed for one of the sandwiches; he was very hungry and had not eaten since the day before – prior to his beating by the Irish hooligans.

"Excuse me, sir, you may want to close that shutter. I have seen three passengers in this past week have their clothes catch fire from the sparks given off by the engine," the news butcher exaggerated.

"Are you serious?" Eli already wanted this journey to end and was beginning to understand why the passenger to his right hand side slept. He wanted to avoid all possibility of further communication with anyone aside from the dark haired young girl opposite.

The blond-haired news butcher stood in front of them, presumably waiting for an order. Eli was agitated upon seeing a smile grow on both the face of the young girl and the boy. She blushed as the boy handed her a small package. "This is a gift for you. I think you will like it. I made it myself." The girl carefully unwrapped the paper to reveal a square of chocolate.

Eli was angered by the effrontery of the rail worker. "Have you not other cars to serve? I think we no longer need anything from you!"

The girl scowled at Eli. She was not happy with his interference. The boy winked at her and left, laughing out loud as he departed the car. Eli felt tension rising within his body, as if he was about to lose control. That would not be desirable. He slumped down in his seat, following the lead of the man who sat to his right, but hoping not to have a similar trail of saliva pooling on his shoulder when he woke. To Eli, the man was disgusting and should be ashamed of himself.

Pulling his red scarf loosely around his face, Eli closed his eyes tight, eventually drifting off into a dream. During his slumber, he dreamt of Jacob and Nancy. In the dream, the three of them were down in the harbour on Sable Island on a crisp, sunny winter's day. A deep snow blanketed the bay and they were throwing snowballs at him, their exuberant laughter sending plumes of white vapour skyward from their happy faces. As his two friends turned toward him, he saw, with horror, their faces had transformed into demons, ready to drag him to some unknown perdition. He woke with a jolt from the nightmare, sweat covering his brow. He suddenly felt ill-at-ease.

As they arrived in Hyannis, Eli had completely forgotten about following the young girl. She herself may never have known how close she was to a most unsavoury encounter.

Stepping onto the platform, Eli spied the news butcher deep in conversation with an older man, presumably his boss. Pausing, he gave the boy one last, lingering look as he moved effortlessly through the steam spouting wildly from the train's dark engine. The platform was now empty, as the blond news butcher made his way past the standing locomotion. As his footsteps echoed along the wooden timbers, he noticed something lying on the floor just ahead. Reaching down, he casually picked up a bright red scarf. He thought it must have fallen from the shoulders of a female passenger and, as it was very nice, decided to keep it rather than hand it into the ticket office.

28

Jacob Makes a Decision

SOMETIMES DECISIONS ARE REACHED EASILY, SOMETIMES, not so much. The choice that lay before Jacob was, in many ways, one of the most daunting of his life. The eccentric Mr Wilson had told him of Eli's visit but, surprisingly, had not gone into too many details concerning what was said. Wilson was perhaps quite protective of the James's family secret after all. He did, however, confirm what Jacob had already suspected, that Eli was heading for Boston on the Yarmouth ferry. Would this mean that Jacob would have to travel to America to continue the pursuit? Or was it time to simply give up?

The ticket office of the Yarmouth Ferry Company was full, not of potential passengers, but of law enforcement officers and company representatives. The mood in the room was grave. Three people sat together behind a large desk; Susan Isner, a chap wearing the distinctive uniform of a ferry captain, and another, larger man, who looked ill-at–ease. In front of them stood a group of five serious-looking individuals, who spewed forth a volley of questions.

"So who exactly was the last to see Mary-Beth alive?"

"Can you account for all the passengers, and were they all questioned before departing?"

"Why doesn't the young girl speak?"

The captain was fending off the suggestion that he had not followed company procedures. He had taken a very defensive tone, as he was fully aware that drownings, under any circumstances, were the full responsibility of a ship's captain. He was also insinuating that it was the fault of the dead Isner girl, who had been in a restricted area during the storm. He cast a guilty look at Susan Isner, embarrassed that he had forgotten that she was present as he cast his aspersions.

Charles Cope raised his hands aloft. "Ok, I've heard plenty. I have enough of a picture to decide if my department will be pursuing this matter further."

"From our perspective, we believe the girl's death to be accidental and also that Captain Watson is not implicated in any wrongdoing," said a man in a grey suit standing next to the policeman. Ernst Young was a senior figure of the Yarmouth Ferry Company. He had arrived to clear this mess up as quickly and efficiently as was possible. He was keen to ensure the company's good name was preserved. The fledgling ferry service was under great pressure from its shareholders to be successful, and a substantial amount of monies had been invested into what many considered a risky operation.

"Then the matter is finished," said Cope.

"It is most certainly not," said the large man, Mr Isner,

who was sat next to his daughter. "We cannot sweep these events under the carpet, and I will not allow blame to be apportioned to my little girl. That is just plain wrong. Besides, not one person has explained to me how it is that my other daughter can be physically attacked on a ferry without anyone being held responsible. What do you intend to do about this, officer?"

This statement prompted resumption of the heated discussion.

A steady rain leaked through laden clouds. The small amount of snow that lay at sporadic intervals along the steep slope that led to the ferry terminal had frozen hard. The resulting black ice made it virtually impossible to maintain an even footing as Jacob and Thomsen – trying to stay upright – gingerly approached the terminal office.

Once inside, the two men instantly became aware of the tension. Arguments were rebounding amongst the serious-looking faces. Jacob quickly took note of a small girl sat at the end of the large desk. She sat quietly, her eyes looking down at her hands as the others continued to shout at each other. Jacob and Thomsen took a seat towards the rear of the waiting area. Susan stiffened as she became aware of their presence, looking directly into Jacob's eyes for just a second before returning her gaze to her hands, resting on the desk.

Susan Isner had not said a word since she had been attacked. Ashen-faced, she had listened to the men for more than two hours as they argued about what exactly had happened during the voyage to Portland.

Suddenly, without warning, she stood up, cleared her throat and began to talk, "It was not Mary-Beth's fault. He pushed her over, I know he did."

They all fell silent. "What did you say?" said Cope.

"He attacked me and my sister saw him. He would have known she would tell everyone what he had done."

"This girl travelled in the pilothouse with me and would not say who attacked her, and as such, seeing as we couldn't detain everyone who was on board, we had to let them all go," said Captain Watson, keen to ensure everyone knew that he had acted professionally. "What was I to do, having a witness who wouldn't be a witness? I am sorry, Miss Isner, sorry that you had such a horrible experience on my boat, sorry you lost your sister, but you wouldn't let me help you."

"He may be listening to us right now," quavered Susan. "He told me he would kill me if I said anything, cut me in my sleep. I am so scared, but I cannot have the blame put on Mary-Beth. She wouldn't have even been out on the deck if it were not for her trying to keep me away from him. It is all my fault," said Susan, her voice breaking with emotion.

Her father reached over and put his arms around his frail young daughter.

"Who are you referring to, and do you know his name?" asked Cope.

"Jacob Madder, that's who attacked me and, I am certain, killed my sister." She burst into tears as the words spilled from her lips. She had held so much in and to finally say his name was a relief. She cared no more about his threats; she just wanted it to be over and to return home.

From the back of the room, Jacob leapt from his seat and shouted, "I know Jacob Madder, and he definitely didn't attack this poor girl, nor kill her sister, but I do have an idea who did."

"How do you know, that young man?" said Cope.

"Because I am Jacob Madder."

"Arrest that man, officer," said Ernst Young.

Charles Cope headed towards Jacob. "Stand still, Jacob Madder."

Thomsen immediately stepped in front of the policeman, protecting Jacob. "Wait a minute, and let's not jump to conclusions here," he said, with as much authority as he could muster.

"Stand back there, this is no business of yours."

"Just ask the girl if I am the man who attacked her," said Jacob. "I know who it was, and we are wasting time,"

"That's not Jacob Madder!" shouted Susan Isner.

"Then who are you exactly?" Officer Cope bore the look of someone wholly confused.

"I am Jacob Madder, and I know the person responsible for this. He is, or I mean, was, my best friend."

The policeman rubbed his chin. "Are you implying that you have something to hide?"

"No sir, I have nothing to hide. I am telling you that Eli James is now responsible for three deaths and one attack and the police must act now!"

"You would say that, wouldn't you?"

"This is madness," said Thomsen, impatiently. "Clearly the girl doesn't know Jacob, and I would add that he was travelling with me from Halifax this past week. It is safe to assume that he couldn't have been in two places at once, could he?"

Once the group had finally accepted that Jacob Madder wasn't responsible for attacking the Isner sisters, discussions led on to what to do next. As far as Charles Cope was concerned, as little as possible. The assumption was that Eli would head for the sparsely-populated regions, perhaps the logging outposts of New Hampshire. He could be anywhere, and there was a real possibility that he would never be found.

"Your friend has been clever; in some ways, you have to admire him," said Cope.

"I would keep that opinion to yourself, officer. There are many who would find such a thought offensive," said Jacob. He was annoyed that anyone, least of all a police officer, could admire Eli.

The fact remained, however, that he had demonstrated a level of deception that belied his years, in order to facilitate his escape. Eli had insisted that the name of Jacob Madder was included on the list of paying passengers intending to return to Yarmouth. It had been relatively easy for him to arrange, as many workers travelled between the two countries looking for temporary work, especially at a time when the fishing season was finished. The officials in the terminal offices seemed ambivalent as to what documentation was required to travel and work in the lumber mills of Maine and New Hampshire. These were very early days for the ferry service, and there was a lot of confusion as to the exact procedures to be followed.

Jacob was frustrated. The trail had gone cold, yet he was still convinced that if he chose to go to Maine he would find Eli.

"Thomsen, I have to go over to Maine. I still have just enough of the money Father Laybolt gave me to pay for it. I must go."

"But what then, Jacob? The money will run out and you can't chase him forever. The time is right to end this, now everyone knows who is behind these horrors."

"No, Thomsen, I can't. What about Nancy? What about Eve and this poor girl he killed on the ferry? He will do it again. I think he's developing a taste for killing and I have to stop him. For them as much as for me."

"Jacob, stop. Please listen to me. You trust me, don't you?" said Thomsen, whilst placing his large hands on top of Jacob's slender shoulders. "You have to let him go, for now. It could take ten years searching New England for him, and look at us. We are in no fit state to carry on. I know it seems wrong and you must know that I will help you in any way I can, but we must leave it to the authorities now. Eli will one day be found out for who he really is."

As he listened to his friend, Jacob caught a glimpse of his

own reflection in the large mirror on the wall of the terminal waiting room. He tried to focus; he didn't recognise the person looking back at him. It was his first look at himself since he had left Sable, weeks ago, and travelling from one end of the province to the other had taken a great toll on his body. He had aged, changed; the face before him was that of an older man, gaunt and in need of rest. It dawned on him that he had not considered how he could carry on chasing Eli over land and seas. That would take time and money. In turn, such a task took planning. He vowed to one day resume the search for Eli. One way or another, he felt it was his responsibility to finally catch his one-time friend. He owed this much to all the lives Eli had destroyed.

Thomsen suggested going straight back to Sable Island to clear his name and sort out any outstanding family business. Jacob reluctantly agreed, although it would be three further months before he finally returned there. He still presumed his father was killed in the Saxby Gale, so would only return when it suited him. In his opinion, there was no rush, no-one he needed to see on Sable. They could think what they wanted, it didn't matter anymore.

Consequently, he decided to spend the harshest part of the winter at Eve's house in the woods. It seemed that now that he had time to actually reflect on what had happened, he was sent to a dark place. Being distracted, as he was by travelling the length and breadth of Nova Scotia, had occupied his mind and now the reality that two of his dearest friends had been brutally murdered finally sank in.

Thomsen remained close, having taken a room nearby in Chester. It was as if he was waiting for Jacob to finally banish some of the horrible memories and be able to move on to a new chapter in his life.

During their final few days in Yarmouth, Thomsen had spoken at great length to Charles Cope, who had been head, for just three months, of the small police department stationed there. The townsfolk of Yarmouth, following a public meeting in October 1869, had hired Cope. He was a straight-talking man with limited communication skills, a trait they had already witnessed first-hand. But no other candidates for the position had come forward, so Cope, with his modest abilities, had been the only option.

Thomsen was trying to convince Officer Cope to remain active in the investigation of the three murders, by linking them to one killer. This was a time, however, before the Mounted Police, and the local police were wholly uninterested in matters beyond the town's border. Cope was therefore only interested in the drowning, and he had reported it to be a tragic accident rather than waste his time acting on a stranger's suspicions of foul play. The perpetrator was in America anyway, so it was not his problem. Cope did, however, offer Thomsen some advice by suggesting that they contact a certain D. W. Johnson, an American currently in Halifax.

Johnson had written to every regional police official in Nova Scotia, looking to establish a new type of police department, one that covered all of the Maritimes by sharing information and expertise. Charles Cope would not be responding to the request. He did, however, suggest that Johnson may be just the man to help Jacob. Once again, this would allow Cope to avoid causing any actual work for himself.

Thomsen wouldn't tell Jacob that any further involvement in the hunt for Eli by local law enforcement was going to be minimal at best and most probably non-existent.

During one particularly long week, when Jacob, still living at Eve's house, had just wanted to be alone to finally grieve, Thomsen travelled to Halifax. He arranged to meet with the American, Johnson, as Charles Cope had suggested. Johnson was enthusiastic and open to any discussion concerning unsolved cases and the sharing of information. It was a radical way of working and one that ultimately would fail, politics being politics when trying to work between two nations. The pioneering law enforcement academy in Boston, however, would prove a great success and established the sharing of information between different regions.

Thomsen felt comfortable putting forward the possibility that Jacob should undergo – when he was ready – initial police training in America. The training would cover many aspects of modern police thinking and successful candidates would most likely be able to forge a career in either Canada or America. Jacob would, in Thomsen's opinion, be an asset to any program. he was a young man of high morals and knew what was right and wrong.

Johnson was already troubled by the loosely-controlled movement of criminals between the coastal towns and cities of both Canada and America. As such, he said that he would consider Jacob and Thomsen for enrolment at his new purpose-built academy in Melrose, Boston. If they were successful, then he had an opportunity for them. He suggested that it may prove advantageous for his team to include someone familiar with life on the many small islands in the area and who was, more importantly, able to communicate with a suspicious population.

29

Two Memorials

THE AXE FELL HEAVILY ON THE beautiful, waxed wood of the boat, a harbinger marking the end of its sailing days. Splinters and dust flew into the air like startled birds, rising only to drift slowly back to Earth in descending circles. Although the temperature was steady at ten below and there was a thick covering of snow, sweat poured from Jacob's brow as he toiled. He had no sentimentality for destroying a boat that was foisted upon him by his father. What had to be done would be done; a symbolic gesture, for Nancy.

The guilt had finally left him during the final leg of his journey back to the island. Jacob hoped that Eli would be hounded by a darkness that would make his life miserable. He vowed to one day track him down. The police could not be trusted to investigate further. As far as they were concerned, Eli was not a Canadian problem anymore. There were also many who still believed that Eli had perished on the steamship that sank on its way to Liverpool. Others still suspected Jacob had a hand in the deaths of the three young women, no matter what Father Laybolt, Susan Isner, or Jacob himself had said.

Chances were that one day, Eli's evil deeds would catch up with him. Jacob was convinced that it would not be long before Eli would be in a position where he would kill again. One of the lessons he had learned since this all began was that nothing was impossible, and one day he hoped to finally confront his wretched friend. He relived the whispered words spoken by Eli as he had departed St Paul's; they were harrowing and still sent chills down his spine. "I will see you again, Jacob, in this world or the next. You can count on it."

Shaking away his anxiety, Jacob returned to the task for which he had come back to Sable. This winter had been long and arduous; April was dawning and the ice and snow would not let up for another month. Even though he had only been away from the island for five months, the feeling of comfort gained from coming home was absent. Certainly, the air carried a familiar smell and nothing had physically changed, yet still Jacob felt like a stranger arriving for a first visit to this most remote outpost. He had changed, in some ways, grown up. The passage from adolescent to adult had been hastened, and Jacob felt different to the boy who had once lived a simple life on Sable Island.

Solemnly, he walked from the boat, along the wooden dock. Joshua Mouton was, as always, sat on a stone wall at the very end of East Street, busy repairing a large lobster pot.

"You still alive, old man?"

"Get away, you barrel of piss. I know I don't scare you with this anymore, little Jacob Madder." Mouton held his deformed hand aloft as he spoke.

In many ways, this was a most reassuring greeting, as if nothing had changed.

He had returned, albeit temporarily, with a single intention, an obsession if you will. It was not the time to dwell on what had happened to his father, or to take care of selling the family home. Of course, the Sable fishermen were curious to learn what fate would befall them now that a portion of their livelihood lay at Jacob's feet. On the walk up from the harbour he had seen the fishermen he had known for years preparing their boats for a return to the ocean. One break in the weather and they would be off. They, in return, had viewed him suspiciously, not looking him in the eye. They would not yet know that it was his intention to leave Sable for good and free them of any debt to the Madder estate. In his pocket were the legal documents handed to him by Turner & Evans in Lunenburg, outlining the small fortune his father had procured during his time on the island. He cared little for the money. He saw his future in Boston, working alongside Thomsen at the new law enforcement academy in Melrose. As he approached the corner of Young and East Street, his old home looked the same; and the people had certainly acted in the same suspicious way, yet something, no, everything was different. He knew that his time on Sable would be short, and perhaps this would turn out to be his last ever visit to the island.

The wooden gate leading to the small front yard hung precariously on one hinge. It struck Jacob how quickly properties fell into disrepair if they were not looked after. The high winds, laden with salt and harsh temperatures, were cruel to man-made possessions. To the side of the residence his dory sat, winterised now that old man Mouton had returned her home. She waited, ready to be set loose on open water. Jacob ran his finger along her transom; even though her sails were gone, lost to the Atlantic, she was a truly beautiful boat. He had come solely with the purpose of removing the bow and hauling it to the Field of Souls. Once his task on Sable was complete, he would have one final obligation back in Lunenburg.

Hillcrest cemetery on Gallows Hill was to be his father's final resting place. When the day came, there was a small, simple service. Jacob and Thomsen were in attendance at St Norbert's. No fisherman was present as Tom was committed to the earth. A simple inscription was carved on the small stone that marked the grave; 'Tom Madder – died December 27th 1869.'

But even before that day, as Jacob returned to the family home, he felt guilty that he had not shed a tear for his father. He had not been shocked when he was told that his father had, like him, survived the Saxby Gale. Nor when he was told that his father had died after he had been brought back to Sable. Mr Turner had informed him that his father never recovered from his injuries. The general feeling on the island was that his father had simply not had the will to live and had given up. Jacob would miss his father, but not as much as he would long for the company of Nancy or Eve.

Jacob had seen for himself, on that fateful night in October, how some of the memorials were badly damaged, so it mattered little that the wooden bow of his dory was now broken into uneven shards. It would still represent what was intended; the commemoration of his dear friend, Nancy. Jacob thought it not only a fitting monument but also an ending to a terrible chapter of his own life.

Years from now, there would be little concern that Jacob's dory was destroyed by his own hands, rather than by some terrible incident out at sea. The sentiment was the same, and in the end the action was equally cathartic to those left alive; in this instance, young Jacob Madder.

Three planks made up the bow on the dory. The wielding of his axe had broken them halfway down the length of the boat, just beyond the seat that he had occupied during the Saxby Gale. He laid them on the ground beside the broken boat, then went inside the house to find a sharp knife so that he could carve the message he had thought so long about. It would take him twenty minutes to crudely etch out the words, and upon completion he set off for the Field Of Souls with the memorial strapped to an old mare loaned for the purpose.

Constantly undermined by his wife, Robert James was now ready to act. He had followed Jacob from a safe distance, from the corner of Young Street to the Field Of

Souls. He had observed in silence from behind Tanner's memorial as Jacob hammered the broken bow into the solid, stony ground just a few feet away. That Jacob decided to mount Nancy's commemorative wood so close to the cliff's edge gave Robert an interesting opportunity.

In some ways, Jacob had become responsible for his own fate from the moment he had arrived back on the island proclaiming that he was not culpable in the murder of Nancy Haas. Further, he had let it be known that it was Eli who was solely to blame. Now everyone thought Robert's son was a monster. The family name was in ruins, and it was all Jacob's fault. Lisbeth again and again had told him as much.

The hammer came down for one final time. It had taken well over forty strikes to drive the wooden bow into place. Each strike reverberated through Jacob's small frame, yet the sound was lost on the wind. Jacob pushed against his broken bow to ensure that it was steadfast enough to resist the high winds that constantly raged on this exposed coastline, no matter what the season. Stepping back, he re-read the words he had carved – 'Blessed are the pure in heart for they shall see God. Nancy Haas, a daughter of Sable, 1869'. Bowing his head, he closed his eyes and recited the Lord's Prayer.

Robert rushed forward as Jacob, statuesque, reflected on Nancy's short life. Hitting him square on, Robert's greater weight pushed the younger man towards the edge of the cliff. The two rolled on, tumbling like acrobats towards an untimely end. Only fate intervened; as they reached the very edge, the final roll sent Robert over the cliff and a solitary tree root snagged Jacob's leg, preventing him from following. Somehow, he managed to keep a firm grip on Robert's wrists with both hands.

He simply could not hold on any longer. Their eyes met against a backdrop of crashing waves and seagull cries. After what seemed an impossible length of time, Robert James mouthed three words to Jacob and let go. His body hit the surf, and Jacob could have sworn that he was about to be tossed back, to land precariously on the grassy edge nearby. Instead, the next wave engulfed him, his outstretched arms finally disappearing beneath the waves. Jacob detected a big smile across Robert James's face as he was sucked under. Perhaps he smiled because he was finally free of Lisbeth?

Jacob reflected upon Robert's final words. "My Eli lives." He wondered if death and misfortune had finally flown from Sable and its inhabitants.

* * *

The lighthouse at Chatham towered above William Jacobson, formerly Eli, as he approached the entrance. The wind resonated in his ears as he pushed at the large green door, which was already showing signs of weathering. Impressive as the lighthouse was from a distance, it was clear this close up that the construction had been hasty and was of an inferior standard. Inside, the keeper was busy polishing one of the large copper brackets used for reflecting as much light from the oil lantern as possible. He was unaware that he was in grave danger.

Jacobson closed the door behind him, confident that his anonymity was intact, and that he was now free to start the next chapter of his life. The fact that he had now killed three girls, one of whom was his own sister, didn't seem to concern him. Certainly, the old man inside represented no threat to him.

He wondered how long it would be before the dark urge resurfaced and his life would once again be thrown into chaos.

THE END

Epilogue

A LOON CRIED IN LUNENBURG HARBOUR. Jacob was sat in the summer sunshine, looking out towards Blue Rocks, keeping an eye on the boats that manoeuvred about the bay. Harbour seals were following the fishing boats as they returned with holds full of fish. A lone fisherman on one of the largest boats, casually tossing fish guts into the wake behind them, had attracted seal and gull alike in a frenzied search for an easy meal. It was a scene very familiar to those who lived by the ocean. Jacob took one last, lingering look at Lunenburg from the far end of the manmade dock and thought it was a pretty place. The deep-red painted buildings and narrow streets were quaint. He would miss this place, although the excitement of starting a new life in Boston far outweighed a desire to stay in Nova Scotia.

His train was due to leave later that afternoon, so he thought he would take one final walk along King Street and one last look at his father's grave.

From behind Burma Road, John Barnett rushed from his stores to approach Jacob. "I have a letter for you, Jacob Madder. It has been in my stores for two months. I saw you through the window and remembered that this had arrived." He held out the envelope, addressed to 'Jacob c/o Arcadian Stores, Burma Road, Lunenburg – To be delivered by hand.'

"For me? Are you sure?" Jacob took the envelope from Barnett and headed for Hillcrest cemetery one last time.

Sitting on top of the wall in front of the church, he slowly opened the envelope and took out the letter.

My dear friend, Jacob,

I presume you will be surprised to hear from me. I write to you not in the hope of forgiveness but to inform you that, upon reflection, I have decided to forgive you.

You would find it a fruitless task to come and find me because by the time you read this letter I will most surely be deceased. I admit that my death is just, but more so by my own hands than by yours or those of the police.

I hope you are recovered from your adventures – oh, and don't forget, Jacob, I will see you again, when you least expect it. You can count on that.

Goodbye until then,

Eli

Jacob carefully folded the letter into four and placed it deep in his back pocket. Hopping from the wall, he walked slowly into the cemetery, to tell his father what had happened.

TO CATCH A FISHERMAN

A novel by

Peter Hutson-Jones

CHATHAM 1896

Follow Jacob, as another adventure is about to begin. More than two decades have passed since Nancy and Eve were murdered. In his new role in law enforcement, based in Cape Cod, Jacob, whilst investigating a very disturbing murder, stumbles upon a case that will lead him to confront someone from his past.

The second novel in the Jacob Madder series, "To Catch A Fisherman", coming soon...

Printed in Great Britain
by Amazon.co.uk, Ltd.,
Marston Gate.